DON'T B

Gary must have
because at that
at me and grinned.

"I won't bite you unless you bite me first," he said.

I glanced up, about to make some response, and found Gary's face only inches from mine. Suddenly my heart was pounding so hard I felt short of breath. I looked quickly away, confused by my reaction to his nearness. What was the matter with me, anyway? It was all so silly—this was only good old Gary Hadley, and I was only a substitute for his dream girl, Colette.

I forced myself to relax, and for the next few minutes, we swayed back and forth in time to the music. Neither of us said a word. I figured that Gary was concentrating on keeping his feet out of my way. As for me, I couldn't have spoken if my life depended on it. It would have been impossible to carry on a conversation while my insides were turning to mush.

Recent Bantam titles in the Sweet Dreams series. Ask your
bookseller for titles you have missed:

DON'T BET ON LOVE

Chapter One

"**M**olly McKenzie, have I ever told you that you're my favorite sister?" Mark asked, following me into the kitchen and grabbing me around the waist.

Maybe I have a naturally suspicious mind, but I had lived with my twin brother for seventeen whole years, and I recognized the symptoms. Mark was definitely up to no good.

"I'm your *only* sister," I pointed out, unimpressed. "If it's money you want, I haven't got any—you of all people should know that."

Considering the subject closed, I set to work fixing myself an after-school snack. Unfortunately, Mark wasn't finished with me yet. As I poured a glass of milk, he leaned over the counter and snatched a cookie from my paper napkin.

"What makes you think I want money?" he asked between bites. "All I'm asking for is one little favor."

I scowled at him. "That's what I'm afraid of. Your 'little favors' usually turn out to be major headaches! Whatever it is, the answer is no."

"Oh, come on, Moll! You could at least *listen*, you know."

"Okay, I'll listen," I said reluctantly, leaning against the refrigerator door and taking a sip of my milk. "But remember, I'm making no promises."

"Okay. Today in the locker room after PE, some of us—me, Eddie, Gary, and Steve—were just talking. You know, guy stuff . . ."

I groaned. "Spare me the details, please! The more I hear of your 'guy stuff,' the less respect I have for guys."

"You said you were going to listen," Mark reminded me, snatching another cookie.

2

"Anyway, we were talking about girls and who we'd like to take to the prom. Steve will be taking Liz, of course, and Eddie's thinking of asking your friend Jan." He paused. "Gary said he'd like to take . . . Colette Carroll."

"What?" The glass of milk nearly slipped out of my hand. "You've got to be kidding!"

"What's wrong with that?"

"Well, nothing, I guess," I said. "I mean, anybody can dream. But *Gary Hadley?* And *Colette?*"

It wasn't that I had anything against Gary. In fact, he was probably the least offensive of all my brother's friends. But Colette was the reigning beauty of Carson High's junior class, a tall, leggy brunette with a fantastic figure and a fashion-model smile.

"Sure. Why not? Why shouldn't Gary take her to the prom? He's tall, he's athletic, he's—"

"He's hopeless!" I interrupted. "Look, Mark, anybody who thinks Gary has a ghost of a chance with Colette has to be seriously out of touch with reality. He may be poetry in motion on the basketball court, and he's a perfectly nice guy, but in case you haven't

3

noticed, Gary can't walk down the hall without tripping over his own two feet!"

"So? If your feet wore size fourteen shoes, you'd probably trip over them every now and then, too," Mark retorted. "Anyway, Eddie and Steve agree with you. They say Gary doesn't stand a chance with Colette, but—well, to make a long story short, I've got twenty bucks that says my man goes to the prom with Colette Carroll."

"You actually laid *bets* on whether or not Colette would go out with Gary?" I exclaimed. "Mark, how *could* you?"

He grinned. "Easy. If Colette tells Gary to take a hike, I pay Eddie and Steve ten dollars each. If she goes to the prom with him, they each pay *me* ten. What's the big deal?"

"That is despicable!" I fumed. "It doesn't surprise me that you, Eddie, and Steve would do something so disgusting, but I simply can't believe that Gary would go along with it. I thought he had more self-respect than that!"

"Oh, lighten up, Moll," my brother said, laughing. "He's just a young boy in love."

"Yeah, right. What's *your* excuse?"

"I'm just a young boy who stands to lose

twenty bucks if Gary doesn't take Colette to the prom." Mark beamed at me. "And that's where you come in, sister dear."

"What do you mean?" I asked warily. I wasn't at all sure that I wanted to know.

"Well, Gary's a good guy, but even I have to admit he's no ladies' man," Mark began.

I snorted. "You can say *that* again!"

"And you obviously agree that for Gary to get a date with Colette, he's going to need a little help . . ."

"A *little* help?" I repeated. "That has to be the understatement of the year!"

". . . So I volunteered you," Mark went on as though I hadn't spoken.

"You *what*?" I squawked.

Mark gave me his most appealing grin. "Come on, Moll, have a heart. Here's poor Gary so nuts about Colette that he can't even talk to her without getting tongue-tied, so I thought . . ."

"Forget it!" I snapped. "That's *his* problem, not mine. Besides, it seems to me that you'd be better off worrying about your own prom date. Have you asked anybody yet?"

"Nope, and I'm not going to. I'm going stag," he said cheerfully. "I mean, why tie myself down to one girl for the whole evening?"

"What you *really* mean is that no self-respecting girl would go with you," I retorted.

Mark bristled. "Oh, yeah? It just so happens I could have my pick of any girl at Carson High if I wanted, but I *don't*. And speaking of prom dates, has anybody asked *you* yet?" he added slyly.

"No, and there's nobody I'd particularly like to go with, either," I told him. It was the truth. There wasn't a single guy in the junior class I was interested in. "I probably won't go at all."

"Suit yourself," Mark said with a shrug. "But just because you're boycotting the prom doesn't mean you can't help poor Gary get his dream date."

"No! I refuse to have anything to do with this tacky scheme of yours," I said firmly. "Poor Gary will have to fend for himself."

"But, Moll, I sort of promised him you'd do it."

I stared at him. "You had no right to promise any such thing! Anyway, I couldn't help Gary get a date with Colette even if I wanted to. She's in my algebra class, but I hardly know her."

"What difference does that make? You're a girl," Mark pointed out. "You know what girls like in a guy. You could tell Gary how to act so Colette would like him."

"I won't do it, Mark. No way, nohow!"

I threw my paper napkin in the trash, put my dirty glass in the sink, and headed for the door. But before I reached it, Mark said, "You know, Moll, I was just thinking. It sure would be a shame if Mom and Dad found out about that speeding ticket you got last month—especially after you took such pains to pay the fine without having to ask them for money . . ."

His words stopped me in my tracks. He wouldn't tell on me—would he? I spun around and looked at my brother suspiciously, but Mark was the picture of innocence. Sapphire-blue eyes gazed at me from a cherubic face framed by curls the same golden-blond color as my own. Not for the first time, I wondered how such an angelic face could hide such a devious mind. But knowing him as well as I did, I wouldn't put anything past him—including blackmail.

7

"Look, Mark, I told you I'd pay you back as soon as I could," I pleaded. "I've given you half my allowance every week, just like we agreed. If you'll just be patient for a few more weeks, you'll have the rest, I promise."

Mark shook his head sadly. "I don't know, Moll. Sometimes I think I should have told Mom and Dad a long time ago. I worry about your safety," he added in a voice filled with fake concern.

"Oh, Mark, give it a rest!" I said, scowling. "I was going thirty-five in a twenty-mile-per-hour zone. You make it sound like I was drag-racing or something!"

"The law is the law," Mark said piously. "Of course, if you'd just agree to help Gary Hadley . . ."

I gave up. "Okay, you win." I sighed. "What exactly do you want me to do?"

The next day at lunch I asked Jan and Beth, my two best friends, what they thought of Gary Hadley.

Jan looked surprised. "Gary? I don't know," she said. "I never thought much about him at all, to tell the truth. He's okay, I guess. Awfully klutzy, though."

8

"Yeah, but klutzy in a cute sort of way," said Beth. She always tried to find something nice to say about everybody.

"Nobody ever accused him of being good-looking, that's for sure," Jan went on.

"No, but he's not really ugly, either," Beth put in.

"If he asked one of you to the prom, would you go?" I asked.

Frowning, Jan said, "Hmmm. That's a tough call. It would depend on who my other prospects were. Actually, I'm sort of hoping Eddie will ask me."

"Well, *I'd* go with Gary," Beth said. "He may not be handsome from an objective standpoint, but I think he's sweet."

"Easy for you to say," Jan added. "You've already got a date."

Beth beamed. "Yeah, Chris is coming home from college that weekend. He's even going to rent a limo so we won't have to ride in that run-down pickup of his! Isn't that cool?"

"Don't change the subject," I ordered. Then, trying to sound casual, I asked, "Do you think Colette Carroll would ever consider going to the prom with Gary?"

9

There was a moment of stunned silence, and then Jan began to laugh. "Good grief, Molly! What kind of a question is that?"

"Well, *do* you?" I persisted.

"Absolutely not," Jan stated, tossing her long red hair for emphasis. "Colette Carroll wouldn't be caught dead with Gary Hadley!"

My sentiments exactly. Turning to Beth, I asked, "What about you?"

She twisted one light brown curl around her finger, obviously struggling to find something positive to say. "Well—it's not that I don't think Gary is good enough for Colette, or anything. But she's so pretty and popular that she's sure to have dozens of offers, and—"

"We get the picture, Beth," Jan interrupted. "Just answer the question yes or no."

"Well—no," Beth admitted.

I heaved a sigh. "That's exactly what I told Mark. But does he ever listen to me? Oh, no!"

"What does Mark have to do with it?" Beth asked, puzzled.

10

"My idiot brother bet two of his friends twenty dollars that Colette would go to the prom with Gary," I said.

"You're kidding!" Jan rolled her eyes. "What a stupid waste of money!"

"Just what would you consider a *smart* waste of money?" Beth challenged Jan. "I think it's sweet that Mark has so much faith in his friend."

"You wouldn't think it was so sweet if he'd volunteered *you* to turn Gary into Colette Carroll's dream date," I said bitterly.

"He didn't!" Jan gasped.

I nodded. "He did."

"And you actually agreed to do it?" Jan asked, incredulous.

"I had to." I sighed. "I still owe Mark twenty-five dollars for that traffic ticket I got last month. He said if I didn't pay up right away, he'd tell Mom and Dad about it—*unless* I helped him win his bet."

"And is Gary aware of this bet?" asked Beth.

"Yup."

"Well, maybe Mark was just teasing you," Beth suggested. "I mean, he can't expect you to work miracles!"

11

"Oh, can't he? You obviously don't know my brother," I said wearily.

"Cheer up, Molly," Jan said, patting my hand. "You know how guys are—it was probably just a lot of meaningless locker-room talk, and Mark's forgotten all about it by now."

Feeling a little better, I asked, "Do you really think so?"

Both Beth and Jan nodded vigorously, and Beth said, "I'm sure you don't have a thing to worry about."

I certainly hoped they were right!

Chapter Two

All afternoon I thought about what Jan and Beth had said, and by the time I got home from school, I'd almost convinced myself that I had nothing to worry about. After all, the prom was still two months away, and there were plenty of other things going on between now and then. For one thing, we'd be getting our class rings any day now, and Mark, Gary, and the other basketball players would be kept busy for several more weeks with end-of-season games. Mark might be a few minutes older than me, but he wasn't all that different from the two-year-old I some-

13

times baby-sat. He had a short attention span, and it didn't take much to distract him.

But when Mark got home fifteen minutes later, I discovered that it was going to take more than a class ring or basketball games to make him forget about his latest scheme.

"Here he is!" Mark announced, bursting into the den where I sat struggling with my algebra homework. "The newest Casanova of Carson High School—and what a guy! Gary Hadley!"

A moment later, the newest Casanova of Carson High appeared in the doorway—and tripped over the low step leading down into our sunken den.

"Watch out!" Mark warned about two seconds too late.

"Sorry about that," Gary mumbled, awkwardly recovering his balance.

I looked at him with a sinking feeling in the pit of my stomach. He was even less attractive than I had remembered: six and a half feet tall and rail thin, with an unruly mop of thick, reddish-brown hair that was much too long, and a beak of a nose supporting the ugliest glasses known to mankind. Gary Hadley didn't need a girl to transform him; he needed a magician!

"Hi, Molly," he said, squirming uncomfortably under my examination. "Mark said you could get me in shape for the prom. Do you really think Colette might go with me?"

"Do you believe in miracles?" I countered.

"It'll take a miracle, that's for sure," Gary said with a sigh. "Anyway, thanks for your help."

"Save your thanks for Mark," I said curtly. "It was his idea, not mine."

"I'm starving," Mark cut in. "Do you want anything to eat, Gary?"

"No thanks, but I could use something to drink, if it's not too much trouble," Gary said.

"No problem," Mark assured him. "Molly will help me, won't you, Moll?"

Smiling at me with clenched teeth, Mark grabbed my arm and hauled me out of the room and down the hall to the kitchen. Once there, he dropped any pretense of brotherly affection.

"Is it asking too much for you not to be rude?" he snapped angrily.

"Who's being rude?" I asked, lowering my

voice to match his. "I simply told him the truth, that's all."

"Well, you could be a little nicer, you know. After all, Gary's a friend of mine!"

"Oh, he is, is he?" I asked, raising my eyebrows in mock surprise. "It seems to me that if he *really* were your friend, you'd be trying to talk him out of this crazy scheme instead of encouraging him!"

"What's crazy about it? Gary just needs some pointers on how to get his girl, that's all. What's wrong with that?"

"Nothing, if it were anybody else. But *look* at him, Mark! Surely even *you* can see that he's hopeless!"

A slight sound interrupted us, and we both whirled around guiltily to find Gary standing there, shuffling his huge feet uncomfortably. I tried to judge from his expression whether he'd heard my last remark, but his eyes, distorted by the thick lenses of his glasses, were impossible to read.

"Sorry to take so long," Mark said, making a quick recovery. "Do you want soda or iced tea?"

Gary chose soda, and I began to fill a glass with ice, more to avoid conversation with him than from any desire to play hostess. Unfortunately, my brother was wise to my tactics.

"The way I see it, we've still got two months before prom night," Mark said. "That should give you plenty of time to prepare. Now, if you'll excuse me, I'll leave you guys alone to work out the details."

Before I could argue, Mark made a quick exit.

"I thought he was starving," I muttered under my breath.

I filled Gary's glass with soda, then returned the bottle to the pantry. When I came back, Gary was leaning against the kitchen counter with his arms folded, eyeing me intently.

"You really don't want to do this, do you, Molly?" he asked.

All right, I thought. *If he's going to be frank, so am I.*

"No, Gary, I don't," I said.

"Then why did you agree to it?"

"Blackmail," I said grimly. "Mark paid a speeding fine for me, and he won't let me off the hook until I pay him back."

"Gee, I didn't know that. I'm sorry."

17

"It's not your fault," I sighed.

"Maybe if I talked to Mark . . ."

"Absolutely not," I said firmly. "This is between my brother and me. I'm not going to drag you into our family squabbles."

Gary smiled a little at that. "Don't look now, but it seems like I'm already in."

"Maybe so," I admitted, forcing a smile of my own. "I don't have anything against you personally, Gary," I went on. "It's just the principle of the thing. The very idea of betting money on whether or not a girl will go out with a guy is—well, tacky, to say the least."

Gary nodded sheepishly. "I guess maybe you're right. But the bet wasn't my idea, you know. It was Mark's."

"Why doesn't that surprise me?" I wondered aloud. "Still, you could have refused to go along with it."

"Yeah, I guess I could have," Gary admitted. "But to tell you the truth, I kind of liked the idea. Besides, I didn't want to let Mark down after he laid twenty bucks on the line. Let's face it—would *you* bet money on Colette going out with me?"

"But if you don't think he can win, why did you agree to it?" I asked.

"Well, when Mark said you'd help me, I thought maybe there was a chance." A deep flush crept up Gary's neck and spread across his face. "You see, I've—I've been crazy about Colette since the first time I saw her, but she doesn't even know I exist. I mean, why should she? There's nothing special about me at all."

I'd been determined to figure out some way of wiggling out of the deal, but now I began to have second thoughts. I don't know exactly what weakened my resolve. Maybe it was because Gary was so different from the rest of Mark's friends, who all tried to act like they were *very* special.

First there was Eddie, who lettered in three sports and considered himself a sort of superjock. And then there was Steve, who looked like a male model and was more vain about his appearance than most *girls* I knew. As for Mark, he was good-looking, too, and he knew it. He also seemed to think he was some kind of financial wizard. In a world full of guys all trying to act super cool,

Gary's total lack of pretension was a refreshing change.

"Well," I said at last, "I guess it wouldn't hurt to try."

Gary looked at me in amazement. "You mean you'll help me?"

I took a deep breath and resigned myself to the inevitable. "Yes, I'll do it. That is, I'll *try* to do it," I amended hastily. "But remember, no promises."

"Hey, that's great, Molly. . . ." In his enthusiasm, Gary flung out his long arms. One elbow connected with his glass and knocked it over, sending ice cubes and soda streaming across the kitchen counter. "Oops!"

I grabbed a dishtowel and tried to mop it up before it ran onto the floor.

"I'm awfully sorry . . ." Gary began.

"Never mind," I said with a sigh, already regretting my moment of weakness. "It was an accident. It could have happened to anybody—almost."

Gary swung around the counter to help with the cleanup and almost knocked me over as I was just finishing up.

"Sorry," he mumbled.

"Gary, you've got to stop saying you're

sorry all the time," I told him. "If you want Colette Carroll to take you seriously, you have to stop apologizing for being alive!"

Gary looked mildly surprised. "Was I doing that? I'm—"

"Don't say it!" I interrupted, throwing up a hand to stop him. "Come on—we might as well get started."

I poured him another soda, then led the way back to the den. I cleared my books and notebooks off the couch so he could sit down.

"Algebra," I mumbled, stacking up some scattered papers.

"If you're having trouble, I'd be glad to help you," Gary offered. "After all, I owe you one."

"You mean you actually understand this stuff?" I asked, looking at him with new respect.

"Oh, sure! What are you having trouble with?"

Gary had never struck me as any kind of a genius, but since I was barely squeaking by with C's, I couldn't afford to be choosy.

"Factoring polynomials," I said, showing him the problem I'd been working on ever since I'd come home from school. "I've done this thing three times, and I come up with a different answer every time."

For the next twenty minutes we tackled my algebra homework. To my surprise, Gary turned out to be an excellent tutor. He never talked over my head like my algebra teacher sometimes did, and he didn't treat me as if I were stupid when I made dumb mistakes. In fact, he was much nicer to me than I deserved.

"I think I've got it!" I cried triumphantly when the next problem worked out right on the very first try. "Thanks loads, Gary."

He shrugged. "Hey, algebra's no problem— it's *girls* that I can't figure out."

"So, tell me about you and Colette," I prompted him. "If I'm going to try to get you two together, I need some background."

"Well, you know she transferred to Carson High last spring," Gary began, leaning back on the couch with a dreamy expression on his face. "I'll never forget the first time I saw her. It was in driver's ed, and it was my turn to drive. Colette climbed into the backseat and said, 'Well, it looks like we'll be driving partners.' I took one look at her in my rear-view mirror, and when I saw how gorgeous she was, I got so flustered that I put the car in reverse instead of forward and crashed right into the side of a building."

"I remember hearing something about that," I said, trying hard not to laugh.

"Yeah, the whole school heard about it!" Gary said with a rueful smile. "That got Colette's attention, all right." The smile faded. "But then she asked for another driving partner. And she hasn't spoken to me since."

"Well, you can't go on crashing cars just to keep her attention," I pointed out. "Do you have any classes with her this semester?"

"We're both in Mrs. Adamson's fourth period history class, but we sit on opposite sides of the room," Gary said. "Her locker is close to mine, though, so I see her in the hall several times a day."

"You said she doesn't speak to you. Do you speak to *her*?"

"Well, I try," he said. "The only trouble is, she's so beautiful that I get all choked up and can't think of anything to say."

"That's why you've got to plan ahead," I told him. "Start thinking right now of something you can use to begin a conversation. Then when you see Colette in school on Monday, you can go right up to her and say . . ." I paused, waiting expectantly for him to come up with an opening remark.

Gary furrowed his brow, obviously thinking hard. Suddenly he shouted, "How do you think the Lakers will do in the NBA playoffs?"

I groaned. "No, no, *no!*"

Gary looked crushed. "You don't like the Lakers?"

"Forget the Lakers!" I said. "Forget the NBA playoffs! That might be okay for Mark or Eddie or Steve, but *not* for Colette!"

"What *should* I talk about, then?"

"I don't know," I sighed. This was going to be even harder than I had feared. "What do you have in common?"

"Absolutely nothing," Gary said, sighing, too.

"Wrong! You've got a history class in common—use that as a starting point. Talk to her about the assignment or something. Or, if you can't think of anything else to say, talk about the weather," I suggested. "That's always a nice, safe topic."

"Great!" he exclaimed, jumping up from the couch and heading for the door. "I can't wait till Monday! Thanks, Molly—you're a lifesaver!"

"Whoa! Where are you going in such a hurry?" I asked.

"Home! Today's Friday—I've got only two and a half days to think of something to say!"

Waving good-bye, Gary ran out of the room—and tripped over the same step he'd tripped over on his way in.

I sat there shaking my head, both amused and puzzled. Gary was a strange person, all right! On the basketball court he moved with precision and grace, and yet anywhere else, he couldn't walk and chew gum at the same time. He could explain algebra to me, yet he couldn't put together a coherent sentence when his dream girl was around. How on earth was I going to turn him into the kind of boy Colette would fall for? I couldn't help thinking about the musical *My Fair Lady*. Compared to the obstacles I faced, Professor Henry Higgins's task of transforming Eliza Doolittle into an elegant lady was a cinch!

On the other hand, I didn't have to look very far to find examples of awkward, homely-looking guys who had somehow managed to land gorgeous girls. Of course, those guys usually had other attributes that made up for their shortcomings, like style or charisma.

Unfortunately, Gary Hadley had neither.

Chapter Three

The following Monday I waited with Gary in the hall near his locker, keeping a sharp eye out for Colette Carroll.

"Have you got your opening line prepared?" I asked him.

"Well, I thought maybe I'd ask her how she did on last Friday's history test—unless you think that's too personal," he added quickly. "If it is, I could—"

"No, I think that's just fine."

"Do you really think this will work?" he asked nervously. "I've been worrying about it all weekend!"

"Of course it will," I said with more assurance than I really felt. "Now, try to calm down. Remember, you're not asking her for a date or anything. You're just making a little casual conversation. People do it all the time."

Gary swallowed hard. "What if I go blank?"

"If you go blank, you can always fall back on the weather," I reminded him. "Get ready! I see her coming!"

Gary snapped rigidly to attention, all six feet six of him.

"Will you relax?" I hissed. "Try to act natural, like you were stopping by your locker and just happened to run into her."

Having given Gary his last-minute instructions, I took up a post at the water fountain across the hall so I could watch the proceedings from a discreet distance. Out of the corner of my eye I saw Colette approach, her long, dark curls bouncing with every step she took. I bent over the fountain, pretending to take a drink, and when she drew up even with me, I nodded for Gary to make his move. He squared his shoulders and took a jerky step forward.

"H-hi, Colette," he stammered.

27

She paused and looked at him curiously, as if she vaguely recognized him but couldn't remember exactly who he was. "Huh? Oh, hi," she replied without much interest.

"I—uh—I was just wondering . . ." Gary cast wild, desperate eyes in my direction. I nodded again and smiled reassuringly.

"Yes?" Colette prompted him.

"Uh—we've been having lots of weather lately, haven't we?" he blurted out.

Colette looked mildly surprised for a moment, then turned her glamour-girl smile on high beam. "Yes, lately it seems as if we've been having weather *every* day," she agreed, and continued walking down the hall.

Gary shut his eyes and beat his head against the wall. "I can't believe I said that! She must think I'm a total moron!" he moaned.

I hurried over to him before he could knock himself unconscious. "You weren't all that bad," I lied, but Gary refused to be comforted.

"I was *terrible*! What's wrong with me, Molly? Why can't I talk to girls?"

"*I'm* a girl," I pointed out. "You don't seem to have any problem talking to *me*."

"Yeah, but that's different. You're just Mark's sister."

For some reason, that remark upset me. Then I reminded myself that this was only Gary Hadley, and it really didn't matter one bit what he thought of me.

"All you need is a little practice," I insisted. Suddenly I had an inspiration. "Why don't you come over to my house after school? I just thought of a dynamite way to teach you how to carry on a conversation. It'll work like a charm, or your money back."

At that, Gary brightened a little. "Just what I always wanted," he joked feebly. "A fairy godmother with a money-back guarantee!"

"Be sure to come dressed to play basketball," I called after him as he started down the hall.

Gary turned and stared at me. "Dressed to play . . . ? I don't get it."

"You will," I promised. "See you this afternoon!"

For the rest of the day I had a hard time concentrating on my schoolwork. I was sure I had hit upon the perfect way to teach Gary the art of social conversation. All he really needed was a little confidence. And since he couldn't talk to girls, we'd start off with something he *could* do: play basketball.

When the final bell rang that afternoon, I practically ran the three blocks home. I went straight to my room, where I threw off my school clothes and put on boxer shorts and an oversize T-shirt. Then I pulled my hair up into a ponytail, grabbed my tennis shoes, and went downstairs to wait for Gary.

He arrived about fifteen minutes later, dressed in gym shorts and a gray T-shirt bearing the words "Carson H. S. Phys. Ed." in maroon letters. His long legs were incredibly skinny, and his oversize feet in their heavily padded high-tops looked enormous. His goofy glasses were held in place by an elastic strap across the back of his shaggy head.

"Come on in, Gary," I said, opening the door wide. "Let me get Mark's basketball, and we'll start."

Mark had been watching TV in the den, but he heard what I said. "Molly's going to play basketball? This I gotta see!" he crowed, sticking his head out into the hall.

"Oh, no, you won't!" I said firmly. "Besides, I'm not going to play basketball. I'm going to show Gary how to carry on a conversation with it."

"Why would he want to talk to a *basketball*?" Mark asked.

"Would you just cut the clowning and tell me where it is?" I demanded impatiently.

"It's up in my room somewhere. I'll get it for you if you'll let me watch," he offered.

"No way! I'll get it myself."

I started up the stairs with Gary at my heels. When we reached Mark's room, I flung open the door and froze on the threshold. Mark's bed was unmade, and the blue carpet was barely visible underneath mounds of dirty clothes. On top of the cluttered desk was a half-eaten sandwich that was curling at the edges. I shuddered to think how long it might have been there.

"Yuck! No wonder he keeps the door closed," I said, wrinkling my nose in disgust. "If the health department knew about this place, they'd condemn it!"

"Are you sure there's a basketball hiding in here?" Gary asked, peering at the mess.

I shrugged. "There's only one way to find

out. I'll check the closet, and you look under the bed."

As Gary knelt on the floor beside the bed, I gingerly picked my way across the room and opened the closet door. A tennis racket and a baseball mitt tumbled down from an upper shelf, narrowly missing my head. I was just about to push back the row of shirts hanging from the rod, when a sharp cry of pain came from beneath the bed.

"Owww!"

"Gary!" I cried, whirling about in alarm. "What happened?"

A moment later Gary's head emerged, dusty but intact. "I think something bit me," he said, grinning wickedly.

I snatched up the baseball mitt and threw it at him. "You scared me half to death!" I scolded, laughing.

"I did find the ball, though," he said, reaching under the bed and drawing it out.

"Great! Let's leave this pigsty and get started!"

Gary followed me back down the stairs and out the door to the basketball hoop mounted on the front of the garage, where

32

he'd often played with Mark and their friends.

"I still don't see what basketball has to do with talking to Colette," he said.

"They're not so different, really," I told him. "A conversation is like throwing a ball back and forth. You say something to her, she says something back to you, and so on and so forth."

"Like a passing drill?" Gary nodded in understanding. "I think I'm beginning to catch on."

"All right," I said, bouncing the ball once or twice. "Think back to what happened this morning. What was your biggest mistake?"

"Making a first-class fool of myself," Gary replied without hesitation.

I shook my head.

Gary looked seriously alarmed. "You mean I did something *worse*?"

"Well, yes, in a way. Your biggest mistake was asking a yes-or-no question."

"That's bad?"

"It is when you want to start a conversation. You ask the question, Colette says yes or no, and then she leaves. You have to ask her something that requires more than a one-word answer. *Make* her talk to you!"

"Or else she'll take her ball and go home," Gary said with a grin.

"Exactly! Now, let's try it," I said, tossing him the basketball. "I'll be Colette, and you start a conversation with me."

"Okay." Gary dribbled the ball a couple of times, then tossed it back to me. "What do you think of Mrs. Adamson's history class?"

"It's okay, I guess. Her lectures are kind of boring, though," I answered, throwing the ball to him.

"Yeah, but she's easier than Mr. Overton— at least, that's what I've heard." He threw the ball to me.

"I've heard that, too, but I find it hard to believe. What are you going to do your term paper on?" I asked, heaving the ball at him.

"I haven't decided yet. What about you?"

"Me neither," I answered, catching the basketball as it came back.

As we kept tossing the ball back and forth, the questions and answers got sillier and sillier, but I could tell Gary was feeling more at ease with the whole idea.

"Want to go to the prom with me, Colette?"

34

Gary asked at last, firing the ball in my direction.

"Love to," I answered, and hurled the ball back to him.

"Great! Pick you up at seven," he said, and shot the ball over my head at the goal behind me. It bounced once on the rim, then fell in.

"You did it!" I shouted triumphantly.

Gary paused to push his glasses up on the bridge of his nose. "Yeah, I did, didn't I?" he said with a grin, and we both knew he wasn't talking about making the basket.

"See? All you needed was a little practice," I said as we went back into the house. Mark, who was still watching TV, looked up as we entered the den.

"Finished talking to the basketball?" he asked.

"Uh-huh," I answered.

"Did it talk back?"

"Yep," Gary replied. "It said your room is a health hazard, and it wants to come live with me."

"I'm sorry I asked!" Mark stood up, took the ball from Gary, and dribbled it across the floor.

"Mark, you know Mom doesn't like you dribbling in the house," I reminded him.

"Mom's not here, and you can't tell her, because you still owe me twenty-five dollars," Mark answered. Tucking the ball under his arm, he sauntered out of the room.

"See what I have to put up with?" I said to Gary with a sigh. I sat down on the couch and gestured for him to have a seat. "I just had an idea," I told him. "Why don't you eat lunch with me and my friends tomorrow? It'll give you a great opportunity to practice talking to girls."

"I don't know . . ." Gary removed his glasses and began to polish them absently on the tail of his T-shirt.

"Why not?" I asked, warming to the idea. "They won't bite, I promise. Beth loves everybody, and Jan—"

I broke off abruptly as Gary looked up from cleaning his glasses, and for the first time I really saw his eyes. They were the same chestnut brown as his hair, with long, thick lashes most girls would kill for.

I must have looked astonished, because he asked, "Molly? What's wrong?"

"Nothing. It's just—your eyes." I couldn't seem to tear my own eyes away from his.

"What about them?" Gary asked nervously.

"They're beautiful! Why do you keep them hidden?"

"What do you mean?" He put his glasses back on, and the spell was broken.

"*That's* what I mean," I informed him. "They're hidden behind those hideous glasses!"

Gary laughed. "You don't like my glasses, huh? I'll admit, they were made for durability, not style. They're sports frames— unbreakable."

"Have you ever thought about getting different frames for every day?" I asked. "Maybe something a little less—er—bulky?"

Gary shook his head. "It wouldn't work. The lenses are so thick, it takes really sturdy frames to support them."

"What about contact lenses?"

"To tell you the truth, I have a pair at home," he confessed.

"Then why don't you wear them?"

"I used to, except when I played basketball. But then, after the season started, I spent so much time taking them out and putting them back in, it was easier just to wear the glasses and leave the contacts at home."

"But basketball season is almost over now, isn't it?" I persisted.

"Yeah. I guess I just got out of the habit."

"Well, if you want your dream girl to notice you, get back *into* the habit," I ordered him. "Immediately! I want to see you wearing those contacts tomorrow at lunch!"

"Yes, *sir!*" Gary barked, snapping his right hand up in a salute.

That made me feel guilty. "Am I awfully bossy?" I asked.

"Yeah," he said with a grin. "But I don't mind. I'll do anything you say if it'll get me that prom date with Colette."

Chapter Four

"Now, remember," I told Jan and Beth in the cafeteria the next day, "Gary Hadley is going to eat lunch with us, and I want both of you to be nice to him. You know, I think there may be hope for him after all. Just wait till you see him! You're in for the surprise of your life!"

I was so eager for my friends to see Gary without his glasses that I could hardly eat. Instead, I pushed lukewarm macaroni and cheese around on my plate, looking up every time the cafeteria door opened.

I'd been doing that for about ten minutes

when the door opened once more and several kids came in.

"There he is now," Beth said.

I spotted Gary at the same time. But something was wrong. He was wearing his glasses! I slumped back in my chair, bitterly disappointed.

"Amazing," Jan breathed, choking back a giggle. "I never would have recognized him!"

"Will you knock it off, Jan?" I snapped irritably. "It isn't funny!"

I was so impatient to find out what had gone wrong that I could hardly sit still while Gary went through the lunch line. At last he reached the front of the line, paid for his meal, and came directly to our table.

"Hi, Molly," he said sheepishly, folding himself into the empty chair next to mine.

"What happened?" I asked as soon as he sat down. "I thought you were going to wear your contacts!"

"Well," he began, "there's a little problem . . ."

"What *kind* of problem?"

"Last time I took them out and cleaned them, I must have left them soaking in the wrong solution," he mumbled. "When I opened the case this morning to take them out, there was nothing but a sort of film floating on the surface."

"You mean . . . ?"

Gary nodded sadly. "I vaporized them."

"I can't believe you did that." I squawked.

"It's easier than it sounds, Molly, believe me," Beth spoke up. "Something like that happened to me once."

"You wear contacts, too?" Gary asked her.

She nodded. "For about a year now. So does Jan. It's unreal, isn't it? I mean, all the care that goes into those things."

"And once you take the contacts out, you have to put on your glasses, anyway," Gary added.

"Exactly!" Beth agreed, glad to find a kindred spirit. "People with perfect vision just can't understand."

Since I was the only person at the table with twenty-twenty vision, I knew that comment was aimed at me. Without warning, I felt a small stab of resentment against Beth for making me feel like an outsider while she monopolized Gary's attention. But the feeling vanished as soon as it had come, making me ashamed of myself. After all, I had invited

Gary to join us so that he could practice talking to girls, and that's exactly what he was doing.

Now that the ice had been broken, things went well for the rest of the lunch period. Beth was prepared to think the best of Gary from the start, and even Jan, who was considerably more cynical, managed to unbend enough to ask him about the outlook for next year's basketball team. By the time Beth and Jan left the cafeteria, they had won my undying gratitude. As for Gary, a mere two days earlier I never would have thought it possible that he could talk so easily with two girls he hardly knew.

"You were great!" I told him after Beth and Jan were gone. "See? Our basketball practice yesterday really paid off. You kept the conversational ball bouncing back and forth . . ."

I chattered on for quite a while before I realized that I was talking to myself. Gary's attention had drifted to a point across the cafeteria from where we sat. Following his lovesick gaze, I wasn't terribly surprised to discover Colette Carroll sitting in the midst of a group of Carson High's most popular

42

kids. It was kind of touching, in a way. I couldn't help wishing that somebody—not Gary Hadley, of course, but *somebody*— would look at me like that.

"Gary? Are you listening?" I asked, knowing the answer perfectly well. *"Gary?!"*

Gary turned and looked at me as if he'd just remembered that I was there. "Did you say something, Molly?"

"Never mind," I said, shaking my head. "It wasn't important."

Gary was absent the next afternoon because he had an appointment to be fitted for new contacts. After a week of playing fairy godmother, I thought I would be ready for a break, but oddly enough I sort of missed him. During algebra class I decided to take the opportunity to have a few words with Colette myself on Gary's behalf. When the bell rang, I waited for her, and we left the room together.

"What do you think of Mr. Mitchell?" I asked as we walked down the hall, referring to our algebra teacher.

"I try not to think of him at all," Colette

43

replied with a grimace. "I'm terrible at algebra. If I didn't need the math credit, I wouldn't be taking this stupid class."

"I know the feeling," I said, a little surprised to find that I had something in common with the divine Colette Carroll. "But if you ever need a tutor, I know a guy who's really good."

"Oh, really?" Colette asked, looking interested. "Who?"

"Gary Hadley," I said casually.

Colette's delicately arched eyebrows drew together in a puzzled frown. "Who?"

"Gary Hadley," I repeated. "He's in your history class."

Colette's brow cleared. "Oh, now I know who you mean! The tall, gawky guy with the dorky glasses." She gave a short laugh. "I'll keep him in mind, if I ever get *really* desperate!"

As I watched her make her way down the hall, a sudden surge of anger flooded through me. Of course, she hadn't said anything about Gary that I hadn't said myself. But somehow it was different now. At that moment I wished I *could* turn Gary into a real dreamboat, just to show Colette what she was missing!

Gary was back in school the following morning, this time without his glasses. I saw him in the hall, but he walked right past me without speaking. I guessed he had something on his mind—or, rather, some*body*. Colette Carroll, most likely.

"Gary?" I called after him.

He turned quickly at the sound of my voice, and those gorgeous eyes, still so unexpected, hit me with their full force. "Oh, hi, Molly," he said. "I didn't see you."

"So, how was your visit to the doctor?"

"Okay," he answered, falling into step beside me. "Did anything interesting happen while I was out?"

I decided not to mention my brief encounter with Colette. "Are you kidding? Does anything interesting ever happen around here?"

"Last night I had a brilliant idea," Gary announced. "Since I missed history yesterday, I could ask Colette if I can borrow her notes! Think that'll work?"

"I don't see why not," I said without enthusiasm.

He smiled dreamily. "I'll bet even her handwriting is beautiful!"

I was getting pretty sick of hearing about how perfect Colette Carroll was, and I was sorely tempted to tell Gary a thing or two about his precious Colette. But I bit back the nasty remark on the tip of my tongue. It would only hurt his feelings if he knew what she'd said. Besides, he was bound to find out sooner or later that she had absolutely no interest in him whatsoever.

"That's what I'll do," Gary said decisively as we started down the stairs. "I'll go right up to her before class starts and— *aaaggghhh!*"

I watched in horror and several kids shrieked as Gary lost his balance and tumbled headlong down the stairs, his books flying in all directions.

"Gary!" I cried, hurrying down the stairs to where he lay in a tangled heap at the bottom. Dropping to my knees beside him, I asked, "Gary, are you all right?"

"Well, I've been better," he said, cautiously sitting upright on the bottom step.

"What happened?"

"I kind of missed the first step. I guess I didn't see it."

"Didn't see it?" I echoed indignantly. "But you just got new contacts! Where did that doctor of yours get his degree? Mail-order med school?"

"I'm not wearing my contacts," Gary answered, rubbing the back of his head. "They won't be available for two more weeks."

I stared at him. "You mean you've been running around school half blind? How have you managed?"

"Not too great," he confessed. "Once I almost went into the girls' rest room by mistake, and then I got chewed out for not paying attention in class when I couldn't see what was written on the blackboard."

"But if you can't see any better than that, why on earth didn't you just wear your glasses?"

"Well, you said they were ugly, and you seemed to think it was so important to make a big impression on Colette, and—"

"Oh, you'll make a big impression on her when you show up at school in a body cast!"

I said sharply. "What are you trying to do? Kill yourself?"

I guess I came down pretty hard on him— too hard, maybe. But as long as I was scolding Gary, I didn't have to analyze the feeling of sheer terror that had come over me when I saw him fall, or my overwhelming sense of relief when I knew he hadn't been hurt.

"I thought I was doing the right thing," Gary mumbled. "Guess I was wrong."

I had started to gather his scattered books, but something about the tone of Gary's voice made me turn back. With his disheveled hair and long-lashed brown eyes, he looked so much like a sorrowful little boy that all my anger melted away.

"Just take it easy, okay?" I said, smiling. "You don't want to break a leg this close to prom night. How would you dance with Colette?"

"Dance?" Gary looked horrified. "Do you mean I'll have to *dance*?"

"That's what people usually do at a prom, you know," I pointed out.

"Well, yeah, but I don't know how," he confessed. "I thought maybe we could just sit on the sidelines and watch."

"If you try that with Colette, you'll find yourself sitting alone while she dances with everybody else," I said firmly. "Look, since you don't know how to dance, I'll teach you. Come over to my house Saturday morning at about eleven, okay? There's nothing to it, I promise. You'll be surprised at how easy it is."

"I have a feeling *you'll* be the one who's surprised"—Gary sighed—"but if you say so, I guess I'll be there."

He rose stiffly to his feet, and I frowned, noticing the way he winced. "Are you sure you're okay?"

"I'm positive," he said, taking the books I held out to him. "Come on. I'll walk you to class so you can see for yourself that I'm still in one piece."

"But shouldn't you go home and get your glasses?"

"I've got them right here." He reached into his shirt pocket, pulled out his glasses, and inspected them for damage. "How about that?" he remarked, grinning at me as he pushed them up on the bridge of his nose. "These things really *are* unbreakable!"

* * *

49

"Do you mean to tell me that after watching Gary Hadley trip over his own two feet and tumble down a flight of stairs, you volunteered to teach him to *dance*?" Jan asked incredulously when I reported the episode to her and Beth at lunch. "Don't you think that sounds a little dangerous?"

"Not really," I answered. "Not as long as he wears his glasses, anyway."

"Then you think Colette might actually go to the prom with him?" Beth asked eagerly.

I shook my head. "Not a chance."

"Then why bother with the dancing lessons?" Jan put in.

I hesitated for a moment before answering. I'd been asking myself the same question for the past two hours. Finally I said, "I can't tell Gary he's wasting his time on Colette, especially when he's risking life and limb just to get her to notice him. It would break his heart."

"I don't know, Molly," Beth said, frowning. "It might be best to level with him right away. How do you know you're not setting him up for a bigger disappointment later on?"

"I've thought about that," I replied. "But I

promised Gary I'd help him. I can't go back on my word no matter how hopeless it seems. Besides, I feel kind of responsible for him."

Jan spoke up. "Can I tell you what I think?" I had to smile at her question. Nobody had ever been able to stop Jan from speaking her mind before. "I think you're taking the whole thing too personally, Molly. Gary's seventeen years old—he's not a little kid. He's certainly old enough to take care of himself. In my opinion, you ought to be thinking about getting yourself a date for the prom instead of playing cupid for Gary Hadley."

Beth and Jan left the cafeteria fifteen minutes later, leaving me to finish my lunch alone. As always, Jan had made a strong case for her point of view. Maybe she was right. Maybe I was getting too personally involved. That would explain why I'd overreacted, first to Colette's remarks about Gary and then to Gary's fall. As for my own dateless state, I couldn't have cared less.

Gazing across the cafeteria, I saw Colette at her usual table, presiding over a group of the school's "beautiful people." She looked chic and lovely and totally oblivious of the fact that a sweet, clumsy boy had nearly broken his neck in a misguided effort to impress her. I had to admit that Beth was right, too. There was a big difference between building Gary's confidence and raising false hopes.

Lost in thought, I didn't even notice when Eddie and Steve sat down on either side of me until Steve spoke.

"Scouting her out, huh, Molly?" he asked. "How's our man doing, anyway?"

"Well, he's improving," I said slowly. "Of course, that's not saying much—there was plenty of room for improvement. There still is, for that matter."

"So Mark isn't counting his money yet?" Eddie asked, grinning broadly.

I shook my head. "No. I wouldn't count mine, either, if I were you. But I'd say the odds are definitely in your favor."

Steve chuckled. "I tried to warn him, but you know what Mark's like once he gets an idea into his head."

"Yeah, I know," I said, dismissing Mark with a shrug. "But listen, guys, I've been thinking. Let's assume that you two win the bet and Mark pays up. Then what?"

They both looked completely blank.

"What do you mean?" Steve asked.

"What happens to Gary?" I asked earnestly. "He's really crazy about Colette—you know that. If she turns him down, he could really be hurt. How about calling off this stupid bet?"

"No way!" Eddie said. "You're thinking like a girl, Molly."

"Yeah, Molly," Steve added. "Gary's tougher than that. Guys just aren't that sensitive about that sort of thing."

"Well, I guess you know him better than I do," I said. But I wasn't at all sure they did.

Chapter Five

No matter how confused my feelings were, the fact remained that I still owed Mark money for that traffic ticket. Until I paid him off, I'd have to continue with Gary's tutoring. So when Saturday morning rolled around, I collected my allowance from Dad and paid Mark his weekly installment of five dollars. I spent the next hour or so searching through my collection of cassettes for appropriate dance music, and by the time Gary arrived, I was prepared for our lesson.

After locking the door of the den against Mark's prying eyes, I turned on the stereo, popped a tape into the cassette deck, and turned to face my pupil.

"Well, are you ready?" I asked as a pulsing rock 'n' roll beat blasted out of the speakers.

Gary shrugged. "As ready as I'll ever be, I guess. What do I do first?"

So I showed him. Actually, the lesson wasn't nearly as bad as I had been afraid it might be. Gary's size-fourteen feet did tend to get in the way a bit at times, but they didn't do any permanent damage to mine, and Gary had a surprisingly good sense of rhythm. I felt sure that with practice, he wouldn't have anything to be ashamed of on prom night. Of course, he probably wouldn't have Colette Carroll, either, but I certainly wasn't going to bring that up.

"Well, I guess that takes care of it," I told Gary half an hour later. "I think you'll do just fine."

"What about slow dancing?" he asked.

"What about it?"

"Don't they usually have some of that, too?"

"Well, yes, but . . ."

"Then hadn't we better work on it?"

It was a sensible request, but for some

reason I hesitated. "There's really nothing to it, Gary," I told him. "All you have to do is put your arms around her and sway back and forth. It's a lot easier than what we've been doing."

"Maybe so, but it would make me feel a whole lot better if we tried it just once. Isn't there some tape there that we could use?"

"I guess so," I said reluctantly. "Let me look."

I sorted through my collection again until I found a suitable tape, a cassette containing a song called "No One in the World Like You." As I selected the track and pushed the play button, I couldn't help contrasting the slow, romantic ballad to my dance partner. With his shaggy hair and Coke-bottle glasses, Gary certainly fit the title, although he probably wasn't exactly what the song-writer had in mind.

We spent the first few measures of the introduction getting our feet in the proper position and out of each other's way. Once that was settled, Gary put his arms around me and drew me close. Because of the difference in our heights, the top of my head barely reached his shoulder. I had two choices: I could either rest my head against his chest, or hold it at an uncomfortable angle as far away from him as I could get. I chose the latter. Gary must have sensed my uneasiness, because at that moment he looked down at me and grinned.

"I won't bite you unless you bite me first," he said.

I glanced up, about to make some response, and found Gary's face only inches from mine. Suddenly my heart was pounding so hard, I felt short of breath. I looked quickly away, confused by my reaction to his nearness. What was the matter with me, anyway? It was all so silly—this was only good old Gary Hadley, and I was only a substitute for Colette.

I forced myself to relax, and for the next few minutes we swayed back and forth in time to the music. Neither of us said a word. I figured that Gary was concentrating on keeping his feet out of my way. As for me, I couldn't have spoken if my life depended on it. It would have been impossible to carry on a conversation while my insides were turning to mush.

At last the final notes of the song faded

away, but for a moment we just stood there, wrapped in each other's arms.

Suddenly there was a loud pounding on the door. "Aren't you guys finished yet?" Mark demanded from the other side. "The baseball game I wanted to watch came on TV ten minutes ago!"

The spell was broken, and I took a wobbly step backward out of Gary's embrace.

"Anyway, that's how it's done," I said, then hurried to unlock the door.

Mark strode across the den and headed straight for the television. He turned it on and switched channels until he found his game, then planted himself on the couch.

Gary flopped down beside him. "Who's playing?" he asked, apparently unaware that anything unusual had just taken place.

I didn't hear Mark's reply. I was too busy puzzling over the strange sensations I had experienced during the last dance. Remembering the feel of Gary's arms around me, I shivered a little, and the thought occurred to me that Colette Carroll—or any other girl, for that matter—could do a lot worse than going to the prom with Gary Hadley.

But I knew that Colette would never look

twice at him, and it really wasn't fair. Gary was such a nice guy. It was a shame he was so—well, so geeky-looking.

I studied him as he sat watching television with Mark. Gary's clothes were okay, although he would never be the fashion plate that Steve was. Getting his contacts and losing those glasses would be a big improvement, too. Still, there was one other thing that might make a difference—exactly how much of a difference I wasn't sure, but it was worth a shot.

"Gary," I said impulsively, "have you ever thought about getting a really good haircut?"

The following Monday I called Hair Designs to make an appointment for Gary with Ellen, my favorite stylist. After I explained Gary's problem and told Ellen what I had in mind, I made the appointment for Saturday morning. It was a long time to wait, but I had my reasons for scheduling it so far in advance. Gary was supposed to get his contacts Friday afternoon, and I wanted him to show up at school the following Monday with a whole new look.

The week seemed to drag by, but at long

last Saturday arrived. To my dismay, when Gary picked me up at a quarter of ten, he was still wearing his glasses.

Frowning at him as I climbed into his second-hand Toyota, I asked, "What happened to your contacts? Weren't they ready yesterday, or have you vaporized them already?"

"I have them right here," Gary said, patting the breast pocket of his shirt. "It's a new prescription, and I'm not used to it yet. I thought I'd put them in later. Where is this place we're going to, anyway?"

I gave him directions, and soon we were walking into Hair Designs. The bell over the door jangled merrily as we entered the shop, and Ellen came out of the back room to greet us.

"Hi, Ellen," I said loudly over the rock music that was blaring in the waiting room. "This is Gary Hadley, the one I told you about on the phone."

She studied his shaggy mop critically. "Hmmm. I see what you mean," Ellen said. "How much do you want taken off?"

"Just a trim . . ." Gary began.

"About three inches," I told her.

"Three inches?" Gary echoed in horror. "I won't have any hair left!"

"Yes, you will," Ellen assured him. "Just not as much."

"But I *like* my hair," he protested.

I patted his arm. "I do, too, Gary. It's very nice hair, and I'm sure it would have been very fashionable back in the seventies. But these are the nineties. Besides, if you don't like it, you can always let it grow back."

"But—but . . ."

He kept on "butting" as Ellen led him gently but firmly into the salon. Now there was nothing left for me to do but wait.

I expected to hear a wail of anguish as soon as the hair started to fall, but the music drowned out any sound from the back. I glanced at a couple of magazines, but none of them held my attention for very long, so I started pacing up and down like an expectant father awaiting the birth of his first child.

My nervousness grew with every passing minute. What if I'd made a terrible mistake? What if Gary had really awful ears that would be better covered up? What if . . . ?

"Well, I hope you're satisfied," said a gloomy voice from the doorway to the salon.

I was almost afraid to look. If this whole thing was a disaster, I'd never forgive myself. Taking a deep breath, I turned around very slowly.

There in the doorway stood a very tall, slender boy with reddish-brown hair cropped short on the top and sides, but left long enough in the back to touch his shirt collar. Long, thick lashes framed a pair of eyes almost the same color as his hair, and at the moment those eyes were filled with uncertainty.

I opened my mouth to speak, but I couldn't make a sound. Although I'd hoped for some slight improvement, never in my wildest dreams had I imagined that inside sweet, clumsy Gary was a gorgeous hunk just waiting to be set free!

"Molly, don't look at me like that," he begged. "*Say* something!"

"Oh, Gary," I breathed, finding my voice at last. "You look—you look . . ."

"Like a plucked chicken, right?" he finished for me, nervously rubbing his newly shorn head.

"No!" I exclaimed. "You look fantastic, absolutely *fantastic!*"

Gary blinked. "Are you kidding?"

Still a little dazed, I shook my head. "Believe me, I've never been more serious in my life."

With a tentative smile he said, "Well, I *feel* like a plucked chicken. Are you sure I don't look weird?"

"No, Gary, you do not look weird. Just wait till Colette gets a load of the new, improved Gary Hadley on Monday morning!" I said as we headed for the door. "She'll never know what hit her!"

As Gary started out the door, his head bumped the bell hanging over it, making it jangle wildly. "Oops—sorry about that," he muttered just before he stumbled over the threshold and almost fell.

I couldn't help smiling as I followed him to his car. The "new" Gary Hadley might be a hunk, but there was still a lot of the old Gary Hadley left, and for some reason, I was very glad.

Chapter Six

My family's reactions to Gary's transformation were all that I could have wished for. Since Mom was in the front yard, planting begonias in her beloved flower beds, she was the first to see him.

"Hi, Mom," I called as I hopped out of Gary's car.

She glanced up at me and smiled. "Oh, hello, dear."

Gary got out, too, and strolled over to her. "Hi, Mrs. McKenzie," he said.

Mom stared at him for a moment. *"Gary?"* Her trowel slipped out of her hand and fell to the ground. "Is that really you? Good heavens! I didn't even recognize you!"

"Doesn't he look terrific?" I said proudly. "Say, Mom, is Mark inside?"

"He's helping your dad fix the car," Mom replied, still staring at Gary. "They're both in the garage."

She was only half right. Dad was in the garage, working on the car, but Mark was nowhere in sight, which wasn't really surprising. Whenever there's work to be done, my brother has a habit of disappearing.

"Hi, Dad. Where's Mark?" I asked.

"He's in the house," Dad answered from under the hood. "If you're going inside, will you please send him out here pronto? I sent him in for paper towels, and he seems to have gotten lost."

"Okay, Dad. Come on in, Gary."

"Gary?" Dad looked up from the engine, an amazed expression on his face. "Gary *Hadley*? The same Gary who backed his car over my lawn mower last week?"

"Uh, yes, sir, I'm afraid so," Gary mumbled apologetically.

"Well, you sure don't *look* the same," Dad said, scratching his head. "Don't let it bother you," he added, ducking back under the hood. "The lawn mower incident, I mean. Mark never should have left it in the driveway in the first place."

At that moment the door opened, and Mark entered the garage with a roll of paper towels. "I never should have left—what in the—" He stopped short at the sight of Gary, then slowly circled the spot where we stood, studying Gary from all angles. At last he let out a long, low whistle. "I gotta hand it to you, Moll," he said. "You *did* perform a miracle! I never knew you had it in you."

I grinned. "Actually, it was Ellen at Hair Designs who did it. Everybody's in for a big surprise on Monday."

"Especially Eddie and Steve," Mark chortled. "Are *they* in for a nasty shock! I feel twenty dollars richer already!"

If my own family's reactions were anything to judge by, Gary's new look would be the talk of Carson High School. I could hardly wait until the weekend was over!

As soon as I got to school on Monday morning, I hurried down the crowded corridor in the direction of Gary's locker, eager to see the effect he was having on the other kids. I found him there, all right, surrounded by a group of wide-eyed girls. A bevy of sophomores gazed adoringly up at him while several flirtatious juniors were giggling at something Gary had just said. One of them reached up and ruffled his reddish-brown hair.

Rather than approaching him, I hung back. I knew I should be pleased at Gary's success, but something about the sight of him with all those girls gave me a funny feeling in the pit of my stomach. It wasn't that I was jealous of the attention he was getting—of course not! He certainly deserved it, especially after the way most of the kids at Carson, including me, had either ignored him or made fun of him for the past two and a half years.

At that moment Gary looked up and spotted me standing by the water fountain. From the expression on his face, I could tell that he was far from enjoying his new popularity. When his eyes met mine, they were filled with such relief that it was almost comical.

"Molly! Am I glad to see you!" he exclaimed. He grabbed a maroon and white baseball cap from his locker and jammed it down on his head, concealing his trendy new haircut. Then he pushed his way through the crowd of girls to my side.

"What's with the hat?" I asked, raising my eyebrows.

"I had to put it on in self-defense," he explained. "I'm telling you, Molly, this place is a jungle!"

"You're darned right, it's a jungle," I said with a grin, "and *you're* going on safari." I snatched the bill of the offending cap and twitched it off. "Now, put that thing back in your locker and quit hiding under it!"

"Well, okay," Gary said reluctantly. "If you say so. But I . . ."

His voice trailed off, and his eyes seemed to glaze over as he stared past me down the hall. I didn't have to turn around to know who he was looking at.

"H-hi, Colette," Gary stammered as she approached.

Colette threw him a brief glance. She was about to pass him by, when her huge, dark eyes widened in surprise. I'd never seen anyone do a double take before, but that's what

Colette did. She stared at Gary for a moment, then flashed him a dazzling smile.

"It's Gary, isn't it?" she purred. "Gary Hadley?"

"Uh—yeah," he said, gazing down at her with a dopey grin on his face.

I couldn't believe what I was seeing. True, I was supposed to be grooming Gary for a date with Colette, but in spite of the contacts and the haircut, it had never crossed my mind that she might actually find him attractive. But there she stood, smiling up at him with an unmistakable "come hither" look.

Everything is working out beautifully, I told myself as I watched them walk down the hall together. *Gary will have his dream girl, and Mark will win his twenty dollars.*

So where did that leave me?

I didn't see Gary again until lunchtime, when he had promised to meet me in the cafeteria and give me a progress report. But as he carried his tray past Colette's table on his way to mine, she called to him, then pulled out the vacant chair beside her and patted it invitingly. Gary cast one nervous glance in my direction, then promptly forgot all about me as he sat down beside Colette. She was at her flirtatious best, laughing and tossing her dark brown curls, and Gary was smiling at her dreamily as if she were the only girl in the world.

"Earth to Molly McKenzie! Earth to Molly McKenzie!" Jan called to me from the other side of our table. "I've asked you three times how you did on your algebra test, and I'm still waiting for an answer!"

"Oh—sorry," I mumbled, tearing my eyes away from Colette and Gary. "I guess I wasn't listening."

"You sure weren't," she said, grinning. "You were too busy staring at Gary Hadley. And who can blame you? What a fox! Molly, you asked me once if I would go out with Gary, and I said no. Is it too late to change my mind?"

"You're just like all the other girls in this school!" I snapped irritably. "Where were you last week, before he had a haircut, and when he was still wearing those hideous glasses? You're all so—so *shallow*!"

70

"Well, excuse me for living!" Jan said, taken aback. "What's your problem?"

"Honestly, Jan, can't you see what's happened?" Beth scolded gently. "Molly's fallen in love with the new Gary Hadley."

"I have not!" I cried. "It just makes me furious to see Colette Carroll falling all over him, when just last Friday she wouldn't give him the time of day. Can't he see that she's interested only in his looks? She doesn't care about the *real* Gary at all! Oh, why do boys have to be so *stupid*?"

"Because if they were any smarter, they'd be girls," Jan replied smugly. "You know, Beth," she added, "I think you're right. It sure looks like love to me."

"And *I* think you're both crazy!" I said, blushing to the roots of my hair.

I stormed out of the cafeteria without eating a bite and headed for the girls' room to splash cold water on my burning cheeks. When I came in, I found two girls I slightly knew touching up their makeup before the big mirror over the sinks. Neither of them paid the least bit of attention to me.

"I've got a class with Gary Hadley next period," Ashley told Laurel as she ran a comb through her short brown hair. "Have you *seen* him today? Boy, what a difference!"

"Yeah, but I wouldn't get my hopes up if I were you," Laurel warned her friend. "Colette's already gotten her hooks into him."

"Just my luck," Ashley sighed.

"Give me a break!" I muttered, and both girls' eyebrows shot up in surprise. Giving them a dirty look, I turned on my heel and left the room.

That encounter in the rest room was only the first of many during the week. Everywhere I went, I heard girls talking about "Gorgeous Gary" Hadley. Overnight he had become a charter member of Carson High's in crowd. It was also common knowledge that he was Colette Carroll's own personal property, and I even heard a rumor that Colette was going to give a party in his honor. I knew it was only a matter of time before Gary asked her to the prom, and there was no question in my mind that she would accept.

Meanwhile, my two best friends tried to pretend they were immune to Gary fever. Beth and Jan seemed to walk on eggshells whenever we were together, careful to avoid making any reference to him that might upset me. I knew they were thinking that I was eating my heart out over the new Gary Hadley, but they were dead wrong. I had no interest whatsoever in some overnight wonder.

It was the *old* Gary Hadley I was in love with.

Chapter Seven

Now that I'd finally admitted the truth to myself, Mark's bet was more intolerable than ever. Only now there was a major difference. Before, I was afraid that Colette would turn Gary down and break his heart. Now I was even more afraid that she wouldn't, which would break mine.

The week dragged by, one miserable day at a time, without any mention of whether Gary had asked Colette to the prom. Of course, I didn't expect to hear the news from Gary. I hadn't spent a single minute alone with him since the rest of the world discovered him. Still, I was sure Mark would have been shouting it from the rooftops if he'd won his bet, and so far he hadn't.

Then on Friday afternoon my brother charged into the den, where I sat nibbling popcorn and staring at some dumb rerun on television. Something about the eager look on his face made my heart sink all the way down to my toes. I was sure that my worst nightmare was about to come true.

"What's up?" I asked, hoping I sounded normal.

Instead of answering, Mark said, "Molly, are you doing anything this afternoon?"

"No. Why?"

"Because Gary's coming over in a little while. He says he needs to see you. It's really important."

My heart leapt from my toes right up into my throat. Was it possible that Gary had changed his mind about Colette and realized that I was the girl for him?

"Gary needs to see *me*?" I squeaked.

"Yeah. He's got some questions about table manners. He wants to take Colette to a fancy restaurant on prom night—you know, one of those places where they give you a different fork for every day of the week."

I felt like a deflated balloon. I looked down at the bowl of popcorn in my lap so Mark couldn't see the disappointment in my face. "Sorry. I've got a lot of homework."

"But you just said you weren't busy!" Mark objected.

"I changed my mind," I said, scowling. "Besides, what does Gary need my help for, anyway? If he's taking Colette to the prom, why doesn't *she* help him?"

"Because he hasn't asked her yet," Mark said. Grinning wickedly, he added, "And *she* doesn't owe me money!"

I wasn't sure who I was more annoyed with—Mark for putting me into this impossible situation, or myself for being secretly thrilled at the prospect of seeing Gary alone again, even if it was only to continue preparing him to impress Colette.

At any rate, by the time Gary arrived twenty minutes later, I was ready for him. After looking up formal dining etiquette in an old book of Mom's, I'd set out a single place setting of her best china at one end of the dining room table, flanked by what seemed like an endless array of silverware. I sat at the other end, determined not to let my personal feelings interfere with the task at hand. And if Gary found all those knives, forks, and spoons so intimidating that he lost his nerve and decided not to take Colette out to dinner after all, surely no one could blame me for that.

"All right," I told Gary briskly, motioning for him to sit down. "To your left, you have forks."

"No kidding," he remarked, eyeing them warily. "And a third here."

I consulted Mom's etiquette book. "That's the dessert fork which, as you can see, goes over the plate. The one on the far left is the salad fork, and the one next to the plate is your main dinner fork."

"Got it. But do I really need three different knives, too?"

"We'll get to the knives in a minute," I said. "First, let's take the spoons. The spoon on the saucer is for coffee, the big one beside the plate is the soup spoon, and the little one over the plate is the dessert spoon."

"Hold it!" Gary said. "If I have a dessert *fork*, why do I need a dessert *spoon*?"

I glared at him. "How should I know? That's just what it says in this book."

"Now for the three knives, right?"

"Right. The first one is a salad knife, the next one is for the main course, and the one on the bread and butter plate is for—"

"Don't tell me, let me guess!" Gary interrupted. "Bread and butter! I'll bet all this nonsense was invented back in the Dark Ages by a little old lady with too much time on her hands. What do they do to you if you use the wrong one at a restaurant? Do they toss you out, or just poke you to death with a salad fork?"

"Oh, we haven't gotten to the really good stuff yet," I said, flipping ahead a few pages. "Let's see—there's the salt shovel, the sugar shell, the ice cream knife—"

"Ice cream *knife*?" Gary repeated. "Who eats ice cream with a knife?"

I shrugged. "I guess Emily Post did."

"Well, I'd sure like to ask her a couple of questions," Gary muttered.

"You can't," I informed him. "She's dead."

"And I'll bet I can guess what killed her," he said, waving his butter knife menacingly.

I completely destroyed my businesslike

image by giggling. "Remember, this whole thing was your idea," I pointed out. "You're the one who wants to take Colette to a fancy restaurant."

"Actually, it was Mark's idea," Gary told me. "He seems to think she'll expect it. Personally, I'd rather stick with something that doesn't need forks—like hamburgers and french fries, or pizza."

"Well, if you *don't* want to take Colette to a fancy restaurant, you don't have to," I said. "You shouldn't let Mark push you around."

Gary glanced down at the silverware. "I know, but he's counting on me to win the bet for him," he said, balancing the butter knife on the rim of a wineglass. "This is really important to him."

"And what about you?" I asked seriously. "Isn't it important to you, too?"

"Well, sure," he said. Maybe it was just wishful thinking, but he didn't sound very sure at all. Before I could say so, Gary spoke up again. "Gosh, I wish there were some easy way to keep all these knives and forks straight."

Suddenly I felt ashamed of myself. Until

four days ago, Gary's love for Colette had been every bit as hopeless as my love for him was now. This was his big chance, and if I really cared about him, I should be doing my best to help him, no matter how much it hurt.

"Okay, let's try something else," I said, getting back to business. "Suppose you want to add cream and sugar to your coffee. Which spoon do you use to stir it?"

"This one," Gary said, pointing to the spoon resting on the saucer.

"Very good! Now, suppose the waiter brings your salad, and the pieces of lettuce are too big. What do you use to cut them up?"

Gary studied the two knives beside the plate, muttering, "Eeny, meeny, miney, moe. This one?" He picked up the one closest to the plate.

"Wrong," I said, checking Mom's etiquette book. "That's the entree knife."

He shrugged. "Oh, well, it was a nice try."

"There *is* a way to remember that might be a little easier," I suggested. "Start with the silverware that's farthest from the plate, and work your way in to the middle, course by course. Do you think that might work?"

"Maybe, but I just thought of another way that sounds even better. I'll bet it would be a lot easier to remember if these plates had real food on them." He grinned at me. "Well, how about it?"

"How about what?" I asked warily. If Gary expected me to whip up a multicourse meal so he could practice eating it and impress his dream date, he could just forget it! I might be head over heels in love, but I still had my pride.

"How about us going out to dinner tonight and trying this stuff out for real?"

My heart began to pound so loudly, I was sure Gary could hear it all the way down at the end of the table. "Us? You mean—you and me? Together?"

"I know it's short notice, but I could pick you up at six, if you want to give it a try."

"I—I'll be ready," I managed to reply.

At a quarter of six I sat on the edge of the living room couch, nervously smoothing the full skirt of my favorite turquoise-blue dress.

This is not—repeat not—a date, I kept telling myself. *This is simply a trial run for Gary's prom date with Colette, and you'd better not forget it.* But no matter how often I said it, I couldn't help feeling thrilled.

I almost jumped out of my skin when the doorbell rang promptly at six. Determined not to appear too eager, I forced myself to remain seated and let someone else answer the door.

"Hey, Moll! Gary's here!" Mark bellowed, and a moment later Gary entered the room.

I had never seen him dressed up before. He was wearing a gray suit, a pale pink shirt, and a gray and pink paisley tie. The padded shoulders of his jacket helped to fill out his beanpole frame. Gary looked absolutely wonderful, from his new haircut all the way down to his . . .

"*Reeboks?*" I said, staring at his sneaker-clad feet. Who else would wear sneakers with a suit? "Wouldn't wing tips be more appropriate?"

"I can tell you've never tried to buy shoes for size-fourteen feet," Gary answered with a rueful grin. "I have to take what I can get."

I could have hugged him. Success would never spoil Gary Hadley, that was for sure!

We drove to the Lamplighter, an elegant new restaurant on the other side of town. The parking lot was crowded, but Gary finally found a vacant space marked "One Hour Parking Only."

"This ought to be okay," he said as we got out of the car. "No matter how many forks there are, it shouldn't take more than an hour to eat dinner."

A white-jacketed maître d' met us at the door and led us across the candlelit dining room to a secluded table for two. After we were seated, I opened my enormous menu. My heart sank when I saw the prices printed there. If Gary was willing to shell out that kind of money for a trial run, he must have high hopes for prom night!

I decided to skip the appetizer and selected an entree that I hoped wouldn't strain his budget too much, then gazed wistfully at Gary, who was still absorbed in studying his own menu. In spite of his new look, he would never be handsome in the classic sense of the word, like Steve or Mark. Gary was too long and skinny for one thing, and his nose hadn't shrunk any. If I looked closely enough, I could still find traces of the boy with the shaggy hair and the thick glasses—the boy I had fallen in love with.

Just then Gary looked up from his menu and caught me watching him. "What is it, Molly?" he asked anxiously. "Have I done something wrong already?"

I smiled and shook my head. "Not a thing." Reminding myself of the purpose of this outing, I asked, "So, is Colette going to the prom with you?" I figured he might have invited her after our cutlery session that afternoon.

"I haven't asked her yet. What about you? Have you got a date?"

"I don't think I'll be going," I said as casually as I could. I had a sudden vision of myself at the prom, sitting alone on the sidelines with the other wallflowers while Colette glided across the floor in Gary's arms. It was a pretty bleak prospect.

"Oh, yeah? Have you got other plans?" Gary asked.

I nodded. Of course I did. I planned to do what any red-blooded American girl would do if the boy she loved was in the clutches of another woman—buy a box of chocolates and eat myself into a sugar-induced coma.

We ordered then, and soon our food arrived. It was delicious and the service was excellent, but I was too depressed to enjoy the meal. Gary concentrated on using the proper utensils, and I didn't have to correct him once. But as I was eating my dessert, I noticed that Gary hadn't touched his.

"Don't you like the chocolate cheesecake?" I asked him. "I think it's awfully good."

"I haven't tried it," he confessed. "I can't. I've run out of forks."

We retraced our steps through the entire meal, matching each piece of silverware to the appropriate course. Sure enough, Gary was one fork short. I caught the eye of our waiter, who came to our table in an instant.

"Madame?"

"The gentleman needs a dessert fork," I said. The waiter looked appalled and hurried off to fetch one.

"Hey, you're pretty good at that," Gary said, grinning at me. "I can tell you've had a lot of experience bossing guys around."

I smiled to keep him from seeing how much his remark had stung. So that was what he thought of me! I was just a girl who bossed guys around. I had to admit that I'd certainly bossed *him* around, and look where it had led. If I hadn't forced Gary into changing his image, Colette Carroll still wouldn't know he was alive, and there might have been a chance for me.

The waiter returned with Gary's fork, and we finished our dessert. As we were getting ready to leave, Gary reached for his wallet. Then he looked at me with the oddest expression on his face.

"Molly, do you have any money with you?" he asked in a strange, constricted voice.

"I've got a few dollars and some change," I said, reaching for my purse. "I think I can handle the tip."

Gary laughed, but there was no humor in the sound. "I'm afraid I'm going to need more than that." He swallowed. "A *lot* more."

"Gary? What's wrong?" I asked, alarmed. By this time his face had taken on a sickly greenish cast.

"I don't have my wallet!" he whispered. "I must have left it in my other pants!"

I thought fast. "Don't panic! I remember seeing a pay phone in the lobby as we came in. Go call your parents and ask them to bring your wallet. Here," I added, pressing a quarter into his hand. "You'll need this."

Gary was gone only a couple of minutes. Even before he reached the table, I could tell by his stricken expression that he'd had no luck.

"There was no answer," he reported, "and I just remembered why. My dad's company is having a dinner tonight. He and Mom probably won't be back for hours!"

"I'm sure my parents are home," I said, standing up. "I'll call them right away."

Gary grabbed my arm. "Molly, no! I can't let your family pay for this."

"You can pay them back tomorrow," I said, gently removing his hand from my arm. "Back in a flash."

My luck was no better than Gary's. I got a busy signal, and I was almost positive that Mark was tying up the phone. I hung up, waited a few seconds, and tried again, with the same result. If I could have gotten my hands on my brother at that moment, I would have choked him. I tried two more times without success, so I finally called the operator, intending to ask for an emergency interrupt. But she informed me that nobody was talking on the phone—there was trouble on the line. By that time, several people were waiting to use the phone and giving me some pretty dirty looks. I was forced to admit defeat. I hung up the receiver, collected my quarter, and returned to the dining room.

"Were they home?" Gary asked hopefully.

I sighed. "I don't know. There's something wrong with the phone, so all I got were busy signals."

At that moment our waiter reappeared. "Will there be anything else?" he asked.

Gary and I exchanged helpless looks. Neither of us knew what to do. Finally Gary spoke.

"I'd like to have a word with the manager, please."

Chapter Eight

"Oh, my aching feet!" I moaned two hours later as we left the Lamplighter through the back door. "I can hardly wait to get home and take off these heels!"

Gary took my arm as we crossed the parking lot. He looked very different from the boy who had picked me up earlier that evening. His tie was loosened, his collar unbuttoned, his shirtsleeves were rolled up to the elbow, and he had slung his jacket over one shoulder.

"See? And you laughed at my Reeboks!" he teased. "Seriously, Molly, thanks for helping out. But I wish you had let me call a taxi to take you home."

"How would we have paid for it?" I asked. "Anyway, it's not like I've never washed dishes before, you know."

"Yeah, but there's a difference between washing dishes for a family of four and washing dishes for a whole restaurant full of people," Gary replied. "And you looked so pretty tonight, too."

My heart was too full of pleasure at Gary's compliment to mind his use of the past tense. "Gary, I don't mind," I said softly. "Honestly, I don't."

We had reached the spot where Gary had parked the car, when a man stepped out of the shadows. Moonlight gleamed on the badge he wore, and suddenly I had a sinking feeling that our troubles weren't over yet.

"This your car, son?" the policeman asked.

"Uh—yes, sir," Gary replied.

"Do you realize you've been parked for over three hours in a one-hour zone?" the officer continued.

"To tell the truth, I forgot," Gary admitted. "But there's a perfectly logical explanation . . ."

"Your driver's license is all the explanation

I need." The policeman held out his hand expectantly.

"Oh, right." Gary automatically reached for his back pocket, then remembered his dilemma. "Oh, no!" he groaned, covering his face with his hand.

"What's the matter?" the policeman asked.

"I—uh—I don't have it with me," Gary said. "But I can explain that, too. You see—"

The officer cut him off. "I see that you're illegally parked *and* driving without a license."

"Like I said, I can explain—"

"You'd better save your explanations for the chief, kid." The policeman jerked his thumb in the direction of his squad car. "We're going to the station. You too, miss," he added.

Gary and I were silent during the short drive to the police station. The only sound was the occasional squawk of the two-way radio. Gary sat beside me in the backseat, staring gloomily out the window, his shoulders slumped. All the confidence he'd gained over the past few weeks seemed to have melted away. I was pretty sure he was thinking of Colette, and although I'm not usually a vindictive person, at that moment I found myself hating her.

I gave a little sigh of pure helplessness, and Gary turned at the sound, giving me a slightly forced smile as he reached for my hand. He gave it a quick squeeze, and didn't release it until we arrived at the police station.

Once inside, we were each allowed to make one phone call. Fortunately, we were both able to get through to our parents this time. I hadn't realized just how awkward it would be until I heard Dad's voice on the other end of the line. How do you break the news that your parents have to come and pick you up at the police station?

Somehow I managed a brief explanation, and when I hung up, our arresting officer led us to the desk sergeant on duty.

"Names, please?" the sergeant asked without looking up from the paperwork on his desk.

"Gary Hadley," Gary said.

"Molly McKenzie," I said.

"All right, what happened?" the desk sergeant asked.

"Well, you see—" Gary began, but the sergeant put up a hand to silence him.

"You'll get your turn in a minute." He turned to the policeman who had brought us in. "What's the story, Cummings?"

"At nine twenty-five I got a call from the night manager at Randolph Drugs," Officer Cummings droned. "Earlier this evening, he'd noticed a 1985 Toyota parked in the lot Randolph Drugs shares with the Lamp-lighter restaurant. Said he noticed it because the parking spaces at that end are designated one-hour parking only. When he closed up, the car was still there. I went to check it out, and while I was writing up the ticket, these two came out of the restaurant. Hadley here admits the car is his, but when I asked for a driver's license, he said he didn't have it with him."

"But I can explain—" Gary began again. This time a new voice interrupted him.

"They ought to make that parking lot bigger!"

We turned and saw a seedy-looking middle-aged man who had apparently been listening to Officer Cummings's endless report.

"Yes, sir, they ought to make it *much* bigger!" he said, standing up. "I'll tell you what I'm going to do. First thing in the morning,

I'm going to go to Randolph Drugs. I'm going to hand Mr. Randolph a check, and I'm going to tell him to make that parking lot bigger!"

"What are you doing here, Wilson?" the sergeant asked wearily. "Have you been writing bad checks again?"

"No!" Mr. Wilson said indignantly. "I never wrote a bad check in my life! It's those computers they use at the bank, that's what it is."

"Never mind the computers! You sit there and be quiet while I hear Hadley's explanation."

Mr. Wilson sat down again, and the sergeant turned back to Gary. "All right, Hadley, you were saying?"

"Well, it's sort of a long story," Gary said.

"We've got all night," the sergeant told him. Somehow that didn't sound very reassuring.

"Well, sir, we—Molly and me—we went to dinner at the Lamplighter, and we parked in a one-hour space because we didn't think it would take that long, but when we got ready to leave, I found out I'd left my wallet at home in my other pants, and I didn't have any money and neither did Molly, so we had to wash dishes to pay for our meal because my folks weren't at home, and Molly's phone was out of order, and—"

"Aw, come on, Sarge, have a heart!" Mr. Wilson urged. "The poor kid's been through enough. Let him and his girlfriend go!"

"You stay out of this!" the sergeant warned. "All right, Hadley, what happened next?"

"Well, we finally left about nine-thirty. I'd forgotten all about where we were parked until I saw the policeman, and he wanted to see my driver's license, but I didn't have it, because—"

"Because it was in his other pants!" offered Mr. Wilson.

"Be quiet, Wilson!" the sergeant bellowed.

"So Officer Cummings brought us here," Gary concluded.

Mr. Wilson stood up and whipped out his checkbook. "I like this kid. I'll tell you what I'm going to do, Sarge. I'm going to pay his fine for him. Just tell me how much it is, and I'll write you a check."

"Wilson, your checks aren't worth the paper they're printed on!" the sergeant growled, growing red in the face. "One more word out of you, and I'll write you up for obstructing justice!"

Mr. Wilson lapsed into sulky silence, and the sergeant turned back to Gary. "Were you able to reach your parents when you called just now?"

"Yes, sir," Gary said. "They're on their way."

"Mine are coming, too," I added in case anybody was interested.

"Are they bringing your wallet with them?" the sergeant asked Gary.

"Well, they should be. At least, I asked them to."

"Fine. If you can show me a valid driver's license, I'll tear up both tickets. Meanwhile, I'll have to hold you in custody until your parents arrive."

Officer Cummings led us to a small room he called a holding pen, but it sure looked like a jail cell to me. He stepped back and allowed us to enter, then pulled the door closed behind us. It shut with a loud clang.

I sank down onto the bench that ran along one wall, then took off my high-heeled shoes and stretched my aching legs out in front of me. Gary paced back and forth like a caged animal, running his hands through his hair.

"I kind of like that guy Wilson," I said, making a feeble attempt at conversation. "I have a feeling he'd be a pretty good fellow to have on your side."

Gary smiled slightly but kept on pacing.

"You might as well sit down," I said at last. "You'll wear a path in the floor."

"Yeah, I guess you're right." He sat down beside me on the bench, leaning forward with his elbows propped on his knees and his chin in his hands.

As I watched him, I found myself wishing our parents wouldn't hurry to our rescue too soon. Colette might have Gary tomorrow, but at least for tonight, he was all mine. A night in a jail cell with Gary suddenly seemed wonderfully romantic, and it was definitely something that he would never be able to share with Colette.

"I'm so sorry about all this, Molly," Gary said, breaking the silence. "I can't seem to do anything right!"

"Oh, Gary, please don't apologize." I reached out and touched his arm. "It wasn't your fault. And I thought you were terrific back there at the Lamplighter, talking to the manager." Steeling myself to say the despised name, I added, "I bet Colette would have been proud of you."

Gary gave a humorless laugh. "Yeah, right."

"Well, she should be! After an evening like

97

this, any girl would be proud to go out with you! Look at it this way. How many people know what it's like behind the scenes at the fanciest restaurant in town? How many people get to ride in the back of a squad car? How many people have adventures like these when they go out on dates?"

Too late, I remembered that this was not a date, and lapsed into embarrassed silence.

Gary slipped his arm around my waist. "You're a good sport, Molly," he said softly. And then he bent his head and kissed me lightly on the cheek.

At that moment Officer Cummings reappeared, jingling the keys to our cozy cell. "Hadley and McKenzie, your folks are here," he said.

I reached for my shoes, glad of an excuse to hide my face from Gary before my expression gave me away. A good sport, he'd called me. I didn't want to be a good sport. I wanted to be the girl Gary loved—but Gary loved Colette Carroll.

Chapter Nine

The rest of the evening seemed sort of anti-climactic after all we'd been through. Officer Cummings unlocked the door and led us back to where the sergeant sat, talking to our parents. Gary claimed his wallet as if he were being reunited with a long-lost friend, then presented his driver's license to the sergeant. He studied it for a moment, then looked at Gary intently, as if he weren't quite convinced that the bespectacled, shaggy-haired boy in the photo and the boy standing in front of him were one and the same. Finally satisfied, he returned the driver's license to Gary and tore up the tickets, just as he had promised. Then Gary left with his parents, and I left with mine.

I was quiet during the drive home, but my mind was racing with thoughts of Gary and me—and Colette. The minute Gary had kissed me, I knew I couldn't go on coaching him and then just turn him over to Colette. I would have to tell Mark that from now on Gary was on his own—even if it meant telling Mom and Dad about the speeding ticket. Funny, but that didn't seem nearly as big a deal as it had just a few hours earlier. I guess going to jail has that effect on a person.

It was after eleven o'clock when we finally got back home. I was exhausted and my feet still hurt, but I was determined to settle the whole thing before I went to bed. I followed Mom upstairs to my parents' bedroom and tapped lightly on the open door.

"Mom, can we talk?" I asked timidly.

"Of course, honey," she answered. "But the sergeant explained everything, and your father and I understand that you and Gary weren't to blame. In fact, we think you both handled the situation with a lot of maturity."

"Thanks, Mom," I said, coming into the

room. "I'm glad you understand. But—well, to tell you the truth, this wasn't my first brush with the law."

Mom's eyebrows drew together in a frown. "Oh? What do you mean?"

I sat down on the edge of the bed, then began hesitantly to tell my story. "A while ago—last month, to be exact—I got a ticket for speeding. I wasn't going all that fast, but I knew you and Dad would have probably grounded me, so—well, I decided not to tell you. Mark loaned me the money to pay the fine, and I've been paying him back out of my allowance every week."

"I see," Mom said thoughtfully. "So what made you decide to tell me now?"

"Well, because Mark wanted me to help Gary get a date with Colette Carroll—she's this gorgeous girl at school, and Gary is prime-time in love with her," I said, although the words almost choked me. "Anyway, I didn't want to do it, but Mark threatened to tell you and Dad about the ticket. So all this time I've been helping Gary get ready to ask Colette to go to the prom with him. But I can't do it anymore because he—I mean, I— but he doesn't . . ."

101

I couldn't hold it in any longer. I buried my face in my hands and burst into tears. Mom put her arms around me and held me close.

"I think I can guess the rest," she said gently. "I'm afraid I can't do anything about you and Gary, but tomorrow I'll pay off your debt to Mark, and you can make the rest of your payments to me. But I'm going to have to take your car keys for a while."

"I know," I sniffed. "You might as well ground me on prom night, too. I won't be going anyway."

"The prom is still a month away," Mom said. "A lot can happen in that time. Who knows? You might get an invitation from somebody you like even better than Gary."

"No, I don't think so," I said sadly, rising slowly from the bed. " 'Night, Mom."

"Good night, dear. And I hope you've learned something from all of this."

"I sure have, Mom," I said fervently.

"And that is?" she prompted me.

"Always stay within the posted speed limits, and don't try to hide things from you and Dad. Oh, and one other thing."

"What's that?"

"*Never* borrow money from Mark!"

Then I went to bed with a heavy heart but a clear conscience.

I should have known that my brother would be waiting for me the next morning with plenty of jailbird jokes. I endured it all patiently, "good sport" that I was, until Mark made some wisecrack about how he was going to tease Gary at school on Monday.

"Don't you dare!" I exclaimed. "Gary feels just awful about the whole thing, and if you say one word to him about it, I'll—I'll—" I paused, trying to think of something really awful to threaten him with.

Before I could come up with anything, Mom called from the kitchen, "Mark, will you come here a moment, please?"

Mark disappeared into the kitchen. When he emerged a few minutes later, his blue eyes were blazing with anger.

"Mom just told me everything. I can't believe you did this!" he sputtered. "Just when everything was going so great!"

"Did what?" I asked, although I had a pretty good idea.

"Pulled out on Gary and me like that! How

could you play such a dirty trick on your own brother?"

"I never wanted to do it in the first place," I reminded him.

"Yeah, but lately you and Gary have been thicker than sorghum molasses! How can you leave him in the lurch? I thought you'd gotten to be pretty good friends."

"Well, that just shows how little you know," I said coldly. If Mark ever guessed that I had fallen hopelessly in love with Gary Hadley, I'd never hear the end of it. "We made a deal, that's all, and now the deal is off."

But now I'd have to break the news to Gary, and I definitely wasn't looking forward to it. My only consolation was that I would have all weekend to prepare my speech before facing Gary on Monday.

As it turned out, I didn't have that much time. About halfway through the morning the telephone rang, and Mark went to answer it. A moment later he yelled, "For you, Moll. It's your former cellmate!"

I raced upstairs and took the call on the extension in Mom and Dad's bedroom, hoping that Mark wouldn't listen in. My heart was pounding, and my hand was trembling as I lifted the receiver and held it to my ear.

"Hello?"

"Hi, Molly." Just the sound of Gary's voice made me weak in the knees. "I wanted to call and make sure you were okay, after last night."

"I'm fine," I said, touched and a little amused by his concern. What had he thought might happen to me—a terminal case of dishpan hands? "What about you?"

"Well, I'm afraid my pride is still kind of bruised, but the rest of me is hanging in there. Listen, Molly, are you busy this afternoon? I thought maybe we could go to town and look at tuxes. I need to get my reservation in, and I sure could use your advice."

I took a deep breath. It was now or never. "No, Gary, I'm afraid I can't," I said.

"Then how about tonight?"

"No. I'm sorry, Gary, but I'm not going to be able to help you anymore."

There was a long silence on the other end of the line. When Gary finally spoke, he sounded both stunned and hurt.

"It's because of what happened last night, isn't it? Now you really *do* think I'm hopeless."

"No!". So much had changed since he'd overheard me saying that to Mark that I was horrified at the memory of my own words.

"Then why?"

"Because—well, because you don't need me anymore," I said, unable to keep the sadness out of my voice. "Like I told you last night, any girl would be proud to go out with you."

"Would *you*?"

Would I! How could I possibly answer his question?

"Well, I—if it weren't for—I mean, if only—that is, I . . ."

"Never mind," Gary said, putting a merciful end to my idiotic stammering. "Forget I mentioned it."

Chapter Ten

But of course I couldn't forget. I spent most of the weekend sitting in my room, remembering Gary's kiss and playing "No One in the World Like You" over and over again on my stereo.

I wasn't particularly looking forward to school on Monday morning. Now that I had resigned my position as Gary's personal trainer, there was no reason for us to meet or even to speak to each other. I couldn't imagine that anything unusual or interesting would happen—but I was wrong.

I had just finished taking my books out of

my locker, when I heard someone calling my name. Turning, I saw Colette Carroll hurrying down the hall in my direction. I didn't even know Colette *knew* my name. But bigger surprises were in store.

"Molly, have you heard that I'm giving a party for Gary?" she asked.

"I've heard rumors about it," I answered.

"Well, the rumors are true. It's this Saturday night. How would you like to come?" Colette asked, beaming at me. She seemed to expect me to swoon from the sheer thrill of being invited to one of her oh-so-exclusive gatherings.

Needless to say, I didn't swoon, but I certainly was startled. Why would Colette go out of her way to extend an invitation to a girl she'd hardly spoken to more than half a dozen times all year? It probably had something to do with Gary, but just what, I didn't know.

"I'm not sure if I'm free," I hedged. "I'll have to let you know. What time does it start?"

"Eight o'clock. See you there, I hope." Wiggling her fingers in farewell, Colette continued down the hall.

When I told Beth and Jan at lunch about her invitation, they were as puzzled as I was.

"Colette invited you to her party?" Beth gasped in surprise. "Molly, why?"

"I have no idea," I said. "But I'm sure she has her reasons."

"Yeah, and I'm sure they aren't purely social," Jan agreed. "Have you ever talked to Colette about Gary?"

"Well, a few weeks ago I did tell her that he was a good algebra tutor," I said thoughtfully, "but that was all."

"Algebra?" Jan echoed, raising a skeptical eyebrow. "When I saw her in the hall with Gary right before last period, algebra was the *last* thing on that girl's mind!"

As if on cue, Colette entered the cafeteria, clinging possessively to Gary's arm.

"So what are you going to do about it, Molly?" asked Beth.

Unable to tear my eyes away from Gary and Colette, I watched as they took their places in the cafeteria line. "What *can* I do?" I asked sadly. "It's what I trained him for."

"She meant the party," Jan said, giving me a knowing look. "You *have* got it bad, haven't you?"

I nodded. There was no point in trying to deny what Jan and Beth already knew.

"What about it, Molly?" Beth asked. "Are you going or not?"

"Definitely not," I said.

"Gary might feel more comfortable if some of his old friends were there," Beth suggested. "I mean, he doesn't know Colette's crowd all that well."

Across the cafeteria, Gary held a chair for Colette. She gave him a megawatt smile as she sat down, then quickly scooted her chair closer to his.

"I don't think he'll have much opportunity to be lonely," I said with a sigh.

"Well, hey!" Jan put in brightly. "Who needs Colette and her old party, anyway? Let's all do something together this weekend!"

"Great idea!" Beth agreed. "Where should we go?"

"Where else? The mall!" Jan said. "We can go shopping for prom dresses!"

"Oh, nice going, Jan!" Beth scolded with uncharacteristic sarcasm. "That's just what Molly needs to make her feel better!"

"It's okay," I said, smiling in spite of the

heaviness in my heart. "I'd love to go with you to pick out your gowns. Friday night, or Saturday?"

Beth voted for Saturday, so I wouldn't sit at home brooding all day, but since Jan had a date that afternoon, we settled for Friday. Actually, I had no real desire to go anywhere, especially shopping for prom dresses. Beth was right—it reminded me too much of Gary and Colette, and of Mark's bet, which was looking more like a winner all the time. In fact, I thought wryly, probably the only people who could even come close to understanding the way I felt were Eddie and Steve, each of whom would most likely be ten dollars poorer by prom night.

But I knew Beth and Jan meant well, so on Friday night I pasted on a cheerful smile and crawled into the backseat of Beth's battered VW. As we rode to the mall, Jan chattered away, predicting that I would meet a handsome stranger that very night, a guy who would never fall down the stairs, trip over his own feet, or botch the simplest comments about the weather, and who would never *ever* forget his wallet and land himself and his date in jail. But Jan's fictional dreamboat held no appeal for me at all.

Once inside the mall, the three of us wandered from store to store, alternately admiring and criticizing the dresses we found. Then, as we approached the fountain at the center of the mall, Beth spotted a peacock-blue formal in one of the shop windows.

"That's it!" she cried, pointing at the dress. "The prom dress of my dreams!"

"In Lundquist's?" Jan asked skeptically. "Isn't that a little rich for your blood, not to mention your pocketbook?"

"Probably," Beth admitted. "But I'll have only one junior prom, you know. At least let's see how much it costs!"

"You go ahead," Jan said, sitting down on the low wall surrounding the fountain. "I'm going to wait here and rest my tired feet."

"Tired feet, huh?" Beth echoed skeptically, eyeing a group of boys who had just seated themselves on the other side of the fountain. "What about you, Molly? Do you want to come with me, or do you suddenly have tired feet, too?"

"Sure, I'll come," I said without much enthusiasm, and followed Beth into the shop.

Of course, once we were inside, one thing led to another. Discovering that the dress was twenty-five percent off only made Beth determined to find out if they had it in her size. And when the saleslady brought out one in size seven, nothing would satisfy Beth but to try it on. I waited patiently outside the dressing room, watching in amusement as various articles of Beth's clothing were flung over the door of the cubicle.

At last the door opened, and Beth stuck her head out.

"Molly, can you come here a minute? I want your opinion."

I joined her, and Beth shut the door behind me.

"Well, what do you think?" she asked, striking a pose.

It was hard for me to get very excited about anything concerning the prom, but there was no denying that the dress could have been designed with Beth in mind.

"I think you look terrific in it," I said, and meant it.

"I don't know," Beth said, critically studying her reflection in the mirror. "I think it looked better on the mannequin."

"That's because the mannequin is six feet tall and wears a size five," I said. "Beth, trust me. You look great! That shade really brings out the blue of your eyes, and—"

I had been about to tell her that the dress made her tiny waist look even tinier, but something made me pause in mid-sentence. The dressing room door shook slightly as someone entered the cubicle next to ours. Then the sound of a girl's voice came floating over the dividing wall.

"Colette, this must be the fourth dress you've tried on tonight," the voice complained.

"Fifth," a second voice corrected her friend. This one I recognized. It belonged to Colette Carroll. I glanced at Beth and raised one finger to my lips.

"Why so picky?" the first girl asked. "Does this mean you have a prom date you haven't told me about?"

"Oh, I've got a date, all right," Colette said confidently. "He just doesn't know it yet."

"You mean Gary still hasn't asked you?" A wild hope that he might have changed his mind died with the other girl's next words. "But everybody knows he's crazy about you. What's taking him so long?"

"Bashfulness," Colette answered. "It was cute for a while, but it's beginning to get old. He'll ask me tomorrow night, though. I'll see to that!"

"How?"

"I invited a girl named Molly McKenzie to my party. She's a friend of Gary's, and unless I miss my guess, a while ago she tried to get the two of us together. At the time I thought she must be nuts, but now I think she might be a useful ally to have." I heard a rustling sound—Colette taking off a gown. "No, I don't think I like this dress, either, Lauren. It's just not *me*. Let's go look somewhere else."

I could hear the unseen Lauren grumbling, and a moment later the door creaked open and shut again. Then there was no sound but the canned music playing over the PA system.

So that explained why Colette had invited me to her party! Gary wasn't moving fast enough for her, and she expected me to give him a shove in her direction. Well, maybe I would go to her party after all, but I wouldn't be the "useful ally" Colette was hoping for. I wasn't giving my Gary to her on a silver platter, no way!

"Beth," I said impulsively, "do you mind if we have another look at that sale rack? I just had a sudden urge to buy a party dress."

Chapter Eleven

Because Mom had taken my car keys, I had to ask Mark to give me a ride to Colette's house. To my surprise, he didn't object. In fact, he seemed glad—even eager—to oblige.

"I have a gut feeling about this party, Moll," he told me happily as he drove down the winding roads of Windsor Heights, the expensive subdivision where Colette lived. "Something good is going to happen tonight, I just know it! That money is as good as mine!"

Since I had my own plans for the party, I didn't bother to disillusion him. Instead, I flipped down the visor mirror and gave my appearance one final inspection. I'd done my hair up in a new style and fastened it with pink silk roses to match my dress. I had to admit, I was rather pleased with the result. It made me look almost glamorous, if you didn't count the light scattering of freckles across my nose. Unfortunately, there was nothing I could do about them. I'd discovered years ago that lemon juice really didn't work, and slathering on heavy makeup only made me look like a clown.

And I certainly don't have anything to be ashamed of in the wardrobe department, I thought, glancing down at my dress. I'd found it on the sale rack at Lundquist's, a pale pink creation with a ruffle over one shoulder, a dropped waist, and a short skirt made of three tiers of ruffles. Even at twenty-five percent off, it had cost me my last dime, and once again I'd had to borrow, this time from Beth. She was enough of a romantic to consider it a sound investment, which, in a way, it was. If the dress would help me rescue Gary from Colette's clutches, it would be worth every penny I owed Beth.

Satisfied, I snapped the visor back up just as Mark slowed down in front of a brightly lit colonial-style house with four white columns across the front.

"Well, here we are," he said, wheeling the car into Colette's already crowded driveway. "Even though you've wimped out on our deal, just keep an eye on Gary for me, okay?"

"Don't worry," I said emphatically. "I will!"

I got out of the car and walked up the lighted path to the house, where a rather intimidating woman met me at the front door. I had never met Colette's mother before, but I recognized her instantly. The tall, slender figure, the dark hair and strikingly beautiful features, the slightly haughty manner—they were Colette all over again.

"You'll find Colette's friends out by the pool," Mrs. Carroll said as if she knew instinctively that I was no friend of Colette's. "Just go straight down the center hall and out the French doors."

Obediently, I followed her directions, glancing through open doorways at rooms that made me think of the home decorating magazines Mom sometimes read. When I reached the French doors leading out onto the terrace, I hesitated. The confidence I had felt earlier was beginning to evaporate.

Colette had certainly gone all out on this party. Since the April evening was still too cool for swimming, the pool was covered with flower-shaped candles bobbing on the surface of the water. A string of Japanese lanterns illuminated two refreshment tables set up at one end of the terrace, where a large group of kids had already gathered around to sample the goodies. There were plenty of faces I recognized, but I didn't see a single person I knew well enough to start a conversation with—there was no sign of Colette, or of Gary, either. I stood there in the doorway, feeling awkward and alone, not knowing what to do next.

Instant wallflower, I thought, glancing down at the sparkling surface of the pool. *Just add water and stir.*

At that moment I heard a masculine voice calling my name.

"Molly! Molly McKenzie!"

I turned toward the sound, and saw Steve separate himself from a group of kids and start walking in my direction.

I hurried to meet him. "Steve!" I exclaimed, relieved to see a really familiar face. "What are you doing here? I thought you'd be out with Liz."

"She's away for the weekend," he explained. "But Mark seemed to think that this would be Gary's big night, so when Colette invited me, I decided I'd better protect my investment. I figure when it looks like Gary's about to ask her to the prom, I can push them both into the pool!"

I smiled at his joke, then asked anxiously, "Did Gary say he's going to ask her tonight?"

Steve shrugged. "Not in so many words. To tell you the truth, Gary doesn't seem to want to talk about it at all, and I don't know why. I mean, Colette is his for the asking. Why, just yesterday she—" Steve broke off abruptly, his eyes fixed on some point behind me. "Well, get a load of that!"

I turned to follow his gaze, and saw Gary and Colette framed in the doorway. Gary wore a pale turquoise sport coat, a white open-neck shirt, and dark trousers. I couldn't help noticing how the color of the jacket brought out the red highlights in his hair.

But it was Colette, clinging tightly to his arm, who riveted my attention. She was wearing a clingy silver tunic over black spandex leggings that hugged her slender legs so closely, I was sure she must have been melted and poured into them. In comparison, my pink ruffled dress seemed dowdy and childish. Colette's dark hair was coiled into a topknot high on her head, revealing silver earrings that dangled almost to her shoulders. All my fighting spirit faded away at the sight of her. How could a pug-nosed, freckle-faced blonde possibly compete with *that*?

"That sound you hear is me kissing my ten dollars good-bye," Steve muttered glumly. "Do you want something to eat? The mob around the refreshment tables is beginning to thin out."

Sure enough, most of the kids had left the food and were now gathering around Colette and Gary. Silently, I followed Steve around the edge of the swimming pool to the refreshment tables at the other end of the terrace. I wasn't at all hungry, but anything was better than standing there and watching Colette and her crowd fawn over the very same boy they'd ignored only two weeks earlier.

Although I didn't want to look, my eyes kept swiveling back to Gary as if they had a will of their own. I was too far away to get a really good look, but there was something about the way he was standing beside Colette with his hands dug into his pants pockets that told me something was wrong.

Impulsively I turned to Steve. "What do you think is the matter with Gary?" I whispered.

"What do you mean?" he asked, dipping a corn chip into the bowl of salsa. "He looks okay to me."

"He seems—" I paused, searching for the right word. "Uncomfortable," I said at last.

"Oh, you know how Gary is. He's probably just bashful. Gary's still not used to being the center of attention. Pretty soon he'll loosen up and start enjoying himself."

Steve's explanation sounded reasonable enough, but I wasn't convinced. "No, it's more than that. Gary looks miserable."

"Well, whatever's wrong with him, Colette will fix it," Steve assured me. "Hey, have you tried these cheese straws? They're pretty good."

I let the subject drop, but while I mingled, talked, and even danced a little, I continued to keep an eye on Gary and Colette. They were pretty painful to watch. I saw Colette reaching up to pop a frosted grape into Gary's mouth; Colette perched on Gary's lap, whispering what were probably sweet nothings in his ear; Colette and Gary wrapped in each other's arms, swaying slowly to the music blaring from the stereo. Worst of all, I saw Colette lead Gary to a dark corner, where she reached up to draw his head down to hers.

I decided that if Gary was unhappy, it was only because he was impatient for all of us to go home so he could be alone with Colette. Suddenly the night air felt chilly and damp, the music was much too loud, and I had a splitting headache.

Glancing at my watch, I saw to my dismay that it was only nine o'clock. Mark wouldn't be coming to pick me up until eleven. I wasn't at all sure I could stand two more hours of this nightmare.

I pushed my way through the crowd back to the French doors, wanting to get away from everybody, if only for a minute or two. Once inside the house, I entered the first room I came to, a library, and closed the door behind me.

I hadn't been there very long when I heard

the door open with a faint creak. Turning to see who had come in, I found myself face-to-face with Gary.

He looked as surprised to see me as I was to see him. "Oh, hi, Molly," he said.

Gary looked just as good up close as he had from a distance. But his tie was loosened and a telltale smudge of lipstick stained the corner of his mouth. Unable to bear the sight, I averted my eyes. "Hi" was all I could trust myself to say.

There was a long, awkward silence. Finally Gary spoke again. "Some party, huh?"

"Oh, yeah!" I agreed with an enthusiasm that sounded strained, even to my own ears. "Colette never does anything halfway," I added, then blushed as I remembered the proof of Colette's thoroughness stamped on Gary's mouth.

After another long pause Gary said, "So, I haven't seen you in a while, Molly. How've you been lately?"

"Oh, just fine," I replied brightly. Still trying to avoid looking directly at him, I lowered my gaze to the floor. That's when I noticed the shiny black leather shoes he wore. "You—you got wing tips," I said.

Gary shifted his weight from one large foot to the other, as if his new shoes were a little too tight. "Yeah, well, I figured I'd need them. You know, with the prom and all."

I nodded. "Yeah, I know."

"Uh—you look really nice tonight, Molly," he said. Was it my imagination, or did Gary seem reluctant to go back to the party?

"Thanks," I murmured. "You look nice, too. But—uh—Gary . . ."

"Yeah?"

"Your—your lipstick is smudged."

"My what?" Suddenly Gary's face turned beet red. "Oh, wow!" He took a handkerchief from the inside pocket of his jacket and began to rub at his mouth, but without much success. "Did I get it?"

I shook my head.

"Would you mind?" Gary asked, offering me the handkerchief.

I took it and reached up, dabbing timidly at the corner of his mouth. I hadn't been so close to him since the day of our dancing lesson, and now all those strange sensations I'd felt came flooding back. What would happen if I put my arms around Gary's neck and drew his head down to mine, the way I'd seen Colette do earlier that evening?

I quickly backed away before I did anything stupid. "There," I said. "That did it."

"Thanks." As Gary returned the handkerchief to his pocket, we heard the opening bars of "No One in the World Like You" coming from the stereo outside. "So, Molly, do you want to dance or something?"

A warm glow filled me all the way down to my toes. Gary remembered "our" song! "I'd like that very much," I said, smiling up at him.

He stepped toward me and was about to take my arm, when Colette burst into the room. "Gary! *There* you are! I was wondering if I should send out a search party." Then she turned her 2,000-kilowatt smile on me. "Oh, Molly, don't you look sweet! I do hope we'll have time for a cozy little chat later."

"Gary and I were just about to dance," I said, feeling the evening's only bright spot suddenly grow dim.

"I hate to disappoint you, but I'm claiming all of Gary's slow dances," Colette said, taking his hand and pulling him out of the room. "Hostess's privilege, you know. I'm sure you understand." Glancing over her shoulder, she gave me a broad wink as she led Gary away.

Alone once again in the library, I felt hot tears sting my eyes, and wiped them away angrily. What had I expected, anyway? I was crazy to have come to this party, and even crazier to have imagined I could ever compete with Colette Carroll. As for that "cozy little chat" she'd mentioned, I'd rather die. But there I was, and unless I could figure out some way to escape, there I'd have to stay until Mark arrived to take me home. Controlling my emotions with great effort, I followed Colette and Gary down the hall and out onto the terrace.

"Hey, where'd you disappear to, Molly?" Steve asked, coming over me. "Want to dance?"

On the other side of the pool, Gary and Colette were holding each other close as they moved in time to the music, their reflections dancing among the candles on the surface of the water. I dragged my eyes back to Steve, who was waiting more or less patiently for an answer.

"Thanks, Steve," I said, "but all of a sudden I'm not feeling very well. Would you mind giving me a ride home instead?"

Chapter Twelve

"Thanks for the ride," I said as Steve's car sped through the darkness, taking us farther and farther away from the scene of my misery. "I'm sorry I made you leave the party early, though."

"No problem," he assured me. "Believe me, I was glad to get out of there, and not just because I figure that Eddie and I are going to lose our bet. I wasn't getting any thrill from watching Queen Colette playing games with her latest toy-boy."

"Don't call him that!" I cried hotly.

"Why not?" Steve said with a shrug.

"That's exactly what he is. Poor old Gary! He'll be history the minute somebody better comes along."

That was exactly what I thought myself, but I couldn't be flippant about it the way Steve was. If there were even the tiniest chance that Colette really loved Gary, I would have tried my best to be happy for him. But she was bound to hurt him, and there was nothing whatsoever to be happy about.

"In fact, that's our only hope of winning the bet," Steve continued. "If some super-cool dude shows up soon, maybe she'll ditch Gary before prom night."

"I think that is a disgusting attitude!" I snapped.

"Okay, okay," Steve said, laughing as he stopped the car in front of my house. "I forgot that you've been helping Mark—I guess you have a pretty big stake in this yourself. By the way, there's someone else who needs your help. Eddie's thinking of asking your friend Jan to the prom, and he wants to know if you'd put in a good word for him."

That was the last straw. "Why am I suddenly responsible for finding *everybody* a date for the prom?" I demanded. "Why doesn't somebody find *me* a date? Not that I want one, anyway," I added quickly, "because I'm sick and tired of the whole stupid thing!"

With that, I climbed out of the car and ran into the house.

Nobody was home. Mom and Dad were playing bridge with some friends, and Mark had gone to the movies with Eddie. I was glad, because the last thing I needed was to answer a lot of questions about why I'd left the party so early.

As I turned on the light in my room, I glimpsed my reflection in the mirror over my dresser. The very sight of my expensive pink dress made me feel sick inside. I had thought Mark's bet was crazy, but I had gambled more recklessly than he ever had, and I had lost.

I took off the dress and threw it over a chair. Sooner or later I would have to hang it up, but at that moment I didn't even want to look at it. I ripped the flowers out of my hair, replaced them with a plain rubber band, and put on an old pair of sweatpants and one of Mark's cast-off T-shirts.

131

It was still too early to go to bed, not that I could have even slept, and there's nothing like food to heal a broken heart, or at least anesthetize it, so I went down to the kitchen. I found some brownies that Mom had baked, poured myself a glass of milk, then took them to the den and curled up on the sofa to watch a corny old thriller on TV. Unfortunately, even *The Squid That Ate Manhattan* couldn't keep my mind off Gary. Every time the giant squid's snakelike tentacles twined around a skyscraper, I thought of Colette wrapping her long, slender arms around Gary's neck.

About halfway through the movie, the grandfather clock in the foyer struck eleven. The party would probably be over now, and all the guests would be gone, leaving Gary alone with Colette. . . .

At that moment the doorbell rang, interrupting my bleak thoughts.

"Coming!" I yelled as the bell rang a second time.

Mom and Dad would have their keys, but my brother often forgot his. I braced myself for the inevitable questions, beginning with why I hadn't waited for him to pick me up, and unlocked the door. But when I flung it open, it wasn't Mark who stood there.

"Gary!" I gasped, painfully aware of how messy I looked. "What are you doing here?"

I could have cut out my tongue for my incredible display of rudeness, but Gary didn't seem to notice my bad manners.

"Hi, Molly," he said. "Can I come in?"

Feeling numb, I stepped aside to let him enter. "Mark went to the movies with Eddie," I babbled, "but he should be back any minute . . ."

"I didn't come to see Mark," Gary said. "I came to see you. I looked all over for you at the party, but they said you'd gone. There's something I have to tell you." He looked as awkward and uncomfortable as I felt.

"Is it about—about Colette and the prom?" I asked.

Gary shoved his hands into his pants pockets and looked down at his new shoes. "Well, yeah, in a way."

"She didn't turn you down, did she?" If Colette Carroll had led Gary on just so she could dump him, I would strangle her with my bare hands!

"No, she didn't turn me down," he said. "I

didn't ask her. To tell you the truth, I'm not *going* to ask her."

I had a horrible suspicion that I had fallen asleep in front of *The Squid That Ate Manhattan.* But if this was a dream, I never wanted to wake up. "You're not going to—"

"Look, Molly," Gary interrupted, "I know you've spent an awful lot of time on me, and I don't want you to think I'm not grateful, but this just isn't working out. After Colette started coming on to me, it took me less than three days to figure out that I didn't really care anything about her." He raised his head and looked deep into my eyes. "I know Mark is counting on me to win his bet, but it's my prom, too, and I think I ought to have some say about who I take. Molly, I'm nobody's dream date, and nobody knows that better than you. But—but I love you, and . . ."

Somewhere I was sure I heard a choir of angels begin singing the *Hallelujah Chorus.* "I love you, too," I said softly.

". . . And if you'll just give me a chance, I'll try not to make you wash dishes, or land you in jail, or—what did you just say?"

I smiled radiantly at him. "I said, I love you, too."

Gary stared at me. "But I thought you wanted me to go to the prom with Colette!"

"Only because I thought *you* wanted to go with her! I mean, the dancing lessons, the contacts, the big dinner . . ."

"It might have started out that way, but before long all I really wanted to do was be with you, and maybe prove to you that I wasn't completely hopeless." He shook his head. "Boy, did *that* ever backfire!"

"You don't have to prove anything to me, Gary," I murmured. "I think I've loved you ever since I heard you make that really *pathetic* remark to Colette about the weather!"

"Is that so? Well, what do you know!" A smile slowly began to spread across Gary's face. "I guess I ought to kiss you or something, huh?"

"That would be nice," I breathed, suddenly shy.

Gary moved forward to take me in his arms, and stepped on my toe. "Sorry," he muttered with a self-conscious grin. When he bent down to kiss me, our noses bumped a couple of times before his lips finally found mine. It wasn't the sort of kiss that dreams are made of, but somehow it seemed just right, and it got even better with practice.

In fact, we were still practicing fifteen minutes later, when the sound of the front door opening made us jump apart. Looking up, we saw Mark standing in the doorway, scowling.

"I suppose you realize," he said, finding his voice at last, "that you two just cost me twenty dollars!"

Gary grinned. "Sorry about that, Mark," he said, still holding me tightly around the waist. "But there are limits to a friendship, you know."

"Hmmm," Mark said thoughtfully, his eyes kindling with hope. "Maybe it's not too late. Do you think you guys could keep quiet about this until after the prom? It's only a couple of weeks away, you know, and . . ."

"Nope," Gary said firmly. "Not a chance."

"Aw, come on, Gary!" Mark protested. "After all, if it weren't for me, you two wouldn't have gotten together at all! How about showing a little gratitude?"

I looked up at Gary. "I don't feel *that* grateful. Do you?"

He shook his head. "Not in the least."

"Okay, how's this? What if I give you a share of my winnings?" Mark coaxed. "Gary takes Colette to the prom, and we split the money seventy-thirty! I think it's only fair that I get seventy percent, since I'm the one who—"

"Go to your room, Mark," I said.

"Sixty-forty?"

"Forget it!"

Mark groaned. "All right, all right! Fifty-fifty, and that's my final offer!"

"Good! Now, will you please go away and leave us alone?"

"Sorry, Mark," Gary said, "but there's only one girl I'm taking to the prom—if she'll go with me, that is," he added, smiling down at me.

"Okay, then, be that way!" Mark grumbled as he stomped up the stairs. "See if I ever do any more favors for you!"

"I feel kind of guilty in a way," Gary said after Mark was gone and we were alone again. "We did have a deal, you know."

"Don't worry about Mark," I told him. "By Monday he'll have come up with some new scheme for winning even *more* money. Now, about the prom . . ."

"What about it?"

"What did you mean, *if* I'll go with you?"

"Don't you remember? That night at the Lamplighter, you told me you weren't going because you had other plans."

"I lied," I confessed. "I said that only because I couldn't bear to see you there with Colette."

Smiling, Gary said, "Well, since that's no longer an issue, do you think there's any chance that I could make you change your mind?"

I stood on tiptoe and wrapped my arms around his neck. "I'd be willing to bet on it!"